"So," David said, "tell me about the body you found—the one that disappeared from the beach."

"What?" Alex said sharply.

"You heard me. Tell me about the body." He came toward her, taking a chair near hers. He was close, too close, and she instantly felt wary and, despite herself, unnerved. They'd been apart for a year, and she was still far too familiar with the rugged planes of his face, the bronzed contours of his hands, now folded idly before him.

"What the hell are you doing on my porch? There's a lobby for guests."

"You must have been in a panic."

"I don't know what you're talking about."

"I'm trying to help you out—and save your life."

"If you want to help me out, get off the island."

"Am I making you uneasy?"

"You bet," she told him flatly.

That drew a smile to his lips. "Missed me, huh?"

Dear Reader,

No doubt your summer's already hot, but it's about to get hotter, because *New York Times* bestselling author Heather Graham is back in Silhouette Intimate Moments! *In the Dark* is a riveting, heart-pounding tale of romantic suspense set in the Florida Keys in the middle of a hurricane. It's emotional, sexy and an absolute edge-of-your-seat read. Don't miss it!

FAMILY SECRETS: THE NEXT GENERATION continues with *Triple Dare* by Candace Irvin, featuring a woman in jeopardy and the very special hero who saves her life. *Heir to Danger* is the first in Valerie Parv's CODE OF THE OUTBACK miniseries. Join Princess Shara Najran as she goes on the run to Australia—and straight into the arms of love. Terese Ramin returns with *Shotgun Honeymoon,* a wonderful—and wonderfully suspenseful—marriage-of-inconvenience story. Brenda Harlen has quickly become a must-read author, and *Bulletproof Hearts* will only further her reputation for writing complex, heartfelt page-turners. Finally, welcome back Susan Vaughan, whose *Guarding Laura* is full of both secrets and sensuality.

Enjoy them all, and come back next month for more of the most exciting romance reading around—only from Silhouette Intimate Moments.

Enjoy!

Leslie J. Wainger
Executive Editor

Please address questions and book requests to:
Silhouette Reader Service
U.S.: 3010 Walden Ave., P.O. Box 1325, Buffalo, NY 14269
Canadian: P.O. Box 609, Fort Erie, Ont. L2A 5X3

HEATHER GRAHAM

IN THE DARK

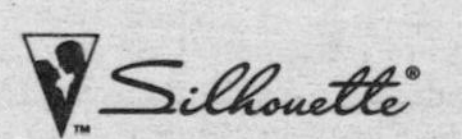

INTIMATE MOMENTS™

Published by Silhouette Books

America's Publisher of Contemporary Romance

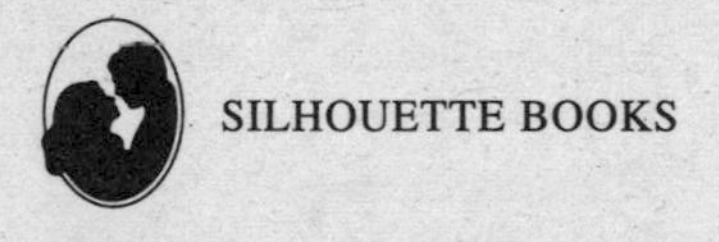

ISBN 0-373-27379-7

IN THE DARK

This edition published by arrangement with Harlequin Books S.A.

Visit Silhouette Books at www.eHarlequin.com

Printed in U.S.A.

Books by Heather Graham

Silhouette Intimate Moments

In the Dark #1309

Books by Heather Graham writing as Heather Graham Pozzessere

Silhouette Intimate Moments

Night Moves #118
The di Medici Bride #132
Double Entendre #145
The Game of Love #165
A Matter of Circumstance #174
Bride of the Tiger #192
All in the Family #205
King of the Castle #220
Strangers in Paradise #225
Angel of Mercy #248
This Rough Magic #260
Lucia in Love #265
Borrowed Angel #293
A Perilous Eden #328
Forever My Love #340
Wedding Bell Blues #352
Snowfire #386
Hatfield and McCoy #416

Silhouette Books

Silhouette Christmas Stories 1991
"The Christmas Bride"

Silhouette Shadows Anthology 1992
"Wilde Imaginings"

Silhouette Shadows
The Last Cavalier

HEATHER GRAHAM

New York Times bestselling author Heather Graham has written more than ninety novels, several of which have been featured by Doubleday Book Club and the Literary Guild. She currently writes for Silhouette Books and MIRA Books, and there are more than twenty million copies of her books in print. Heather lives with her husband and five children in Miami, Florida.

To Mary Stella, with lots of love.

To both the Dolphin Research Organization
and the Theater of the Sea, with thanks.

Prologue

Alex nearly screamed as her foot hit the shell. She choked down the sound just in time but still stumbled, and that was when she fell.

She'd missed the shell, running in the dark. As she lay there, winded from landing hard on the sand, she damned the darkness. In just another few hours, it would be light.

In just a matter of minutes, the eye of the storm would have passed and the hundred-mile winds of Hurricane Dahlia would be picking up again. And here she was, lying next to the water, completely vulnerable.

She rolled quickly, gasping for breath, ready to leap back to her feet. She didn't dare take the time to survey the injury to her foot, as the constant prayer that had been rushing through her mind continued. Please, just let me reach the resort. Please…

A thrashing sound came from the brush behind her.

The killer was close.

She would have to run again, heading for the safety of the resort. Or would even that be safety now?

She needed to reach the resort without being seen, needed to reach the lockbox behind the check-in, where the Smith & Wesson was kept. She was almost certain no one else had taken the gun.

Move! She silently commanded herself. What was she waiting for?

There was no one who could help her, no one she could trust.

She had to depend on only herself, no matter how desperately she wanted to believe in at least one man….

It was then that, so near that she could recognize him despite the darkness, she saw Len Creighton, prone on the sand.

Another body she thought, panic rising in her. Well, she had wondered where he was. And now she knew. He was lying facedown on the sand, a trickle of blood running down his face. The wild surf was breaking over his legs; where he lay surrounded by clumps of seaweed. Already, little crabs were scouring the area, carefully eyeing what they hoped would be their next meal.

She choked back a scream. Above her, the clouds broke. Pale light emerged from the heavens.

And that was when the first man exploded from the bush.

"Alex!" he called. "Get over here."

He stood there, panting for breath, beckoning to her, eyes sharply surveying the area. And he was carrying a speargun, one that had been used on some living creature already—blood dripped from the tip. "Alex, you've got to trust me. Come with me now—quickly."

"No!"

He spun on a dime at the sound of the second voice.

A second man. This one carrying a Glock, which was aimed at the first man.

"Alex, come to me. Get away from him," the newcomer insisted.

The men faced off, staring, each one aware of the weapon the other was carrying.

"Alex!"

This time, she wasn't even sure which man spoke. Once she had trusted them both. One, she had loved before. The other had so nearly seduced her heart in the days just past.

"Alex!"

There was what appeared to be a dead man at her feet. A co-worker. A friend. She should be down on her knees, attempting to find life, however hopeless that might be. But one of the two men facing her was a killer. She couldn't look away. Seconds ticked by, and she stood frozen in place.

Her heart insisted that it couldn't be either man.

Especially not him.

She couldn't think. She could only stand there and stare, eyes going from one man to the other, everything within her soul screaming that neither one of them could be a killer.

But one of them was.

She could feel the ocean lapping over her feet. She knew these waters so well, like the back of her hand.

So did they.

No, not these waters. Not this island. She knew it as few other people could.

There was only one thing she could do, even though it was insanity. The storm might have passed for the moment, but the sea was far from placid. The waves were still deadly. The currents would be merciless.

And yet…

She had no other choice.

She turned to the sea and dove into it, and as she swam for her life, she realized that a few days ago, she wouldn't have believed this.

That was when it had all begun. Just days ago.

She felt the surge of her arms and legs as she strove to put distance between herself and the shore.

Something sped past her in the water. A bullet? A spear?

People always said that in the last seconds of someone's life, their entire past rushed before their eyes.

She wasn't seeing that far back.

Just to that morning, by the dolphin lagoon, when she had found the first body on the beach.

The one that had disappeared.

Chapter 1

"The main thing to remember is that here at Moon Bay, we consider our dolphins our guests. When you're swimming with them, don't turn and stalk them, because, for one thing, they're faster than you can begin to imagine, and they'll disappear on you in seconds flat. And also, they hate it. Let them come to you—and they will. They're here because they're social creatures. We never force them to interact with people—they want to. Any animal in the lagoon knows how to leave the playing arena. And when they choose to leave, we respect their desire to do so. When they come to you naturally, you're free to stroke them as they pass. Try to keep your hands forward of the dorsal fin. And just stroke—don't pound or scratch, okay?"

Alex McCord's voice was smooth and normal—or so

she hoped—as she spoke with the group of eight gathered before her. She had done a lot of smiling, while she first assured the two preteen girls and the teenage boy, who looked like a troublemaker, that she wasn't angry but they would follow the rules. A few of her other smiles had been genuine and directed at two of the five adults rounding out the dive, the father of the boy and the mother of the girls.

Then there were her forced smiles. Her face was beginning to hurt, those smiles were so forced.

Because she just couldn't believe who was here.

The world was filled with islands. And these days the world was even filled with islands that offered a dozen variations of the dolphin experience.

So what on earth was David Denhem doing here, on her island, suddenly showing an extraordinary curiosity regarding her dolphins? Especially when his experiences must reduce her swims to a mom-and-pop outing, since he'd been swimming with great whites at the Great Barrier Reef, photographed whales in the Pacific, fed lemon sharks off Aruba and filmed ray encounters in Grand Cayman. So why was he here? It had been months since she'd seen him, heard from him or even bothered to read any of the news articles regarding him.

But here he was, the ultimate ocean man. Diver, photographer and salvage entrepreneur extraordinaire. Six-two, broad shoulders bronzed, perfect features weathered, deep blue gaze focused on her as if he were fascinated by her every word, even though his questions made it clear he knew as much about dolphins as she did.

She might not have minded so much, except that for

once she had been looking forward to the company of another man—an arresting and attractive man who apparently found her attractive, as well.

John Seymore, an ex–navy SEAL, was looking to set up a dive business in the Keys. Physically, he was like a blond version of David. And his eyes were green, a pleasant, easygoing, light green. Despite his credentials, he'd gone on her morning dive tour the day before, and she'd chatted with him at the Tiki Hut last night and found out that he'd signed on for the dolphin swim, as well. He'd admitted that he knew almost nothing about the creatures but loved them.

She'd had a couple of drinks…she'd danced. She'd gone so far as to imagine sex.

And now…here was David. Distorting the image of a barely formed mirage before it could even begin to find focus. They were divorced. She had every right to envision a life with another man, so the concept of a simple date shouldn't make her feel squeamish. After all, she sincerely doubted that her ex-husband had been sitting around idle for a year.

"They're really the most extraordinary creatures in the world," Laurie Smith, one of Alex's four assistants, piped up. Had she simply stopped speaking, Alex wondered, forcing Laurie to chime in. Actually, Alex was glad Laurie had spoken up. Alex had been afraid that she was beginning to look like a bored tour guide, which wasn't the case at all. She had worked with a number of animals during her career. She had never found any as intelligent, clever and personable as dolphins. Dogs were great; and so were chimps, but dolphins were magical.

"You never feel guilty, as if the dolphins are scientific rats in a lab—except, of course, that entertaining tourists isn't exactly medical research."

That came from the last member of the group, the man to whom she needed to be giving the most serious attention. Hank Adamson. He wasn't as muscled or bronzed as David and John, but he was tall and lithe, wiry, sandy-haired, and wearing the most stylish sunglasses available. He was handsome in a smooth, sleek, electric way and could be the most polite human being on earth. He could also be cruel. He was a local columnist, and he also contributed to travel magazines and tour guides about the area. He could, if he thought it was justified, be savage, ripping apart motels, hotels, restaurants, theme parks and clubs. There was something humorous about his acidic style, which led to his articles being syndicated across the country. Alex found him an irritating bastard, but Jay Galway, manager of the entire Moon Bay facility, was desperate to get a good review from the man.

Adamson had seemed to enjoy the dive-boat activities the day before. She'd been waiting for some kind of an assault, though, since he'd set foot on the island. And here it was.

"The lagoon offers the animals many choices, Mr. Adamson. They can play, or they can retire to their private area. Additionally, our dolphins were all born in captivity, except for Shania, and she was hurt so badly by a boat propeller that she wouldn't have survived in the open sea. We made one attempt to release her, and she came right back. Dolphins are incredibly intelligent creatures, and I believe that they're as interested in learning about our behavior as we are in theirs." She shifted focus to address the group at large. "Let's begin. Is there any particular behavior you've seen or experienced with the dolphins you'd like to try again."

"I want to ride a dolphin," the boy, Zach, said.

"The fin ride. Sure, we can start with that. Would you like to go first?"

"Yeah, can I?"

She smiled. Maybe the kid wasn't a demon after all. Dolphins had a wonderful effect on people. Once, she'd been given a group of "incorrigibles" from a local "special" school. They'd teased and acted like idiots at first. Then they'd gotten into the water and become model citizens.

"Absolutely. One dolphin or two?"

"Two is really cool," David said quietly, offering a slight grin to the boy.

"Two."

"Okay, in the water, front and center. Fins on, no masks or snorkels right now," Alex said.

The others waited as the boy went out into the lagoon and extended his arms as Alex indicated. She signaled to Katy and Sabra, and the two dolphins sleekly obeyed the command, like silver streaks of light sliding beneath the water's surface.

Zach was great, taking a firm hold of each fin and smiling like a two-year-old with an oversize lollipop as the mammals swam him through the water, finishing up by the floating dock, where they were rewarded as they dropped their passenger. Zach was still beaming.

"Better than any ride I've ever been on in my life!" he exclaimed.

"Can I go next?" one of the girls asked. Tess. Cute

little thing, bright eyes, dark hair. Zach had been trying to impress her earlier. Tess opted for one dolphin, and Alex chose Jamie-Boy.

One by one, everyone got to try the fin ride. John Seymore was quieter than the kids, but obviously pleased. Even Hank Adamson—for all his skepticism and the fact that he seemed to be looking for something to condemn—enjoyed his swim.

Alex was afraid that David would either demur—this was pretty tame stuff for him—or do something spectacular. God knew what he might whisper to a dolphin, and what a well-trained, social animal might do in response. But David was well-behaved, looking as smooth and sleek as the creatures themselves as he came out of the water. The only irritating thing was that he and John Seymore seemed to find a tremendous amount to talk about whenever she was busy with the others. Then, during the circle swim, David disappeared beneath the surface for so long that the two parents in the group began to worry that he had drowned.

"Are you sure he's all right?" Ally Conroy, Zach's mother, asked Alex.

"I know him," Alex told the woman, forcing another of those plastic smiles that threatened to break her face. "He can hold his breath almost as long as the dolphins."

David surfaced at last. Macy, the staff photographer, just shrugged at Alex. They made a lot of their research funding by selling people photos of their dolphin experiences, but Alex and Macy both knew David didn't need to buy any photos.

At that point, David and John began talking quietly in the background, as Alex got the others going on their chance for dolphin hugs and smooches. She couldn't hear what the two men were saying, but she was annoyed, and became more so when Hank Adamson joined the conversation. She found them distracting, but had a feeling she'd look foolish if she was to freak out and yell at the lot of them to shut up. It looked like a little testosterone party going. They were probably chatting about diving—in a manly way, of course.

Why did it bother her so much? David was out of her life. No, David would never be out of her life.

The thought was galling. She had been able to see that the relationship wasn't working, that time wasn't going to change the facts about him, her or the situation. And they had split. She didn't regret the decision.

It's just that he was here again now, when she had a lovely minor flirtation going on, the most exciting thing she'd experienced since the divorce. And just because the object of her current affections seemed to be getting on with David as if they were long-lost friends…

"Hey," Zach whispered to her, his eyes alight, "Those guys aren't paying any attention. The girls and I could sneak in and take their hugs, huh?"

She would have loved to agree. But no matter what it looked like Hank Adamson was doing, he was a reporter. One whose writing could influence the fate of Moon Bay. She had to play fair.

"I'd love to give them to you and the girls, but it wouldn't be right."

"Zach, you can take my place."

She hadn't known that David had broken away from his conversation.

She stared at him. “The girls would want an equal opportunity.”

“Hey, I’ll give up my time.” That, amazingly, came from Hank Adamson. He grinned at Alex. “It’s cool watching the kids have fun. Don’t worry—you’re getting a good write-up.”

“I’ll give up my hug, too,” John Seymore told her, shrugging, a dimple going deep.

“Another round for the youngest members of the group, then,” she said.

Finally the time was up. Alex went through her spiel about returning flippers, masks, and snorkels, telling the group where they could rinse off the brine and find further information on dolphins before heading off for whatever their next adventure might be.

John gave her a special smile as he stopped to thank her. “I was figuring I’d do it again, maybe check out a time when the groups weren’t full. I don’t have a thing in the world against hugs. Even from a dolphin.”

She smiled in return, nodding.

“I think I have an in with the dolphin keeper,” he added softly.

“You do,” she assured him.

He turned, walking off. David had been right behind him. He’d undoubtedly heard every word. Now his dark blue eyes were on her enigmatically. She wished he wasn’t even more appealing soaking wet, that thatch of impossibly dark hair over his forehead, bronzed shoulders gleaming. She wished there wasn’t such an irresistibly subtle, too familiar scent about him. Soap, cologne, his natural essence, mingled with the sea and salty air.

"Nice program you've got going," he said. "Thanks."

Then he walked away. He didn't even shake her hand, as the others had. He didn't touch her.

She felt burned.

"Thanks," she returned, though he was already too far away to hear her

"You okay?"

Alex whirled. Laurie was watching her worriedly.

"So hunky-dory I could spit," Alex assured her, causing Laurie to smile.

Then her friend cocked her head, set her hands on her hips and sighed. "Poor baby. Two of the most attractive men I've seen in a long time angling for your attention, and you look as if you've been caught in a bees' nest."

"Trust me, David is not angling for my attention."

"You should have seen the way he was looking at you."

"You were reading it wrong, I guarantee you."

Laurie frowned. "I thought the divorce went smoothly."

"Very smoothly. I don't think he even noticed," Alex told her ruefully. She lifted a hand in vague explanation. "He was in the Caribbean on a boat somewhere when I filed the papers. He didn't call, didn't protest…just sent his attorney with the clear message to let me do whatever I wanted, have whatever I wanted…. I was married, then I wasn't, and it was all so fast, my head was spinning."

"Well, that certainly didn't mean he hated you."

"I never said he hated me."

"Well…want my advice?"

"No."

Laurie grinned. "That's because you've never been to a place like Date Tournament."

"What?"

"I told you I was going the other day," Laurie said impatiently. "It's that new club in Key Largo. They've been doing it all over the country. You go, and you keep changing tables, chatting with different people for about ten minutes each. The idea isn't bad. I mean, there are nice guys out there, not just jerks. Some are heartbroken—like me. And some are just looking. Imagine, the perfect person for me could walk by me in a mall, but we'd never talk. We never see someone and just walk up and say, 'Hey, you're good-looking, the right age, are you straight? Attached? Do you have kids? Do you like the water? We wouldn't last a day if you didn't.' So at Date Tournament, you at least get to meet people who are looking for people. Sexual preference and marital status are all straightened out before you start. You're not stuck believing some jerk in a bar who says he's single, gets more out of the night than a girl set out to give, then apologizes because he has to get home before his wife catches him."

Alex stared at her blankly for a minute. Laurie was beautiful, a natural platinum blonde with a gorgeous smile, charm and spontaneity. It had never really occurred to Alex that her friend had the least difficulty dating. Living at Moon Bay seemed perfect for Alex. She had her own small but atmospheric little cottage, surrounded by subtropical growth—and daily maid service. There was the Tiki Hut off the lagoons for laid-back evenings, buffets in the main house for every meal, a small but well-run bookstore and every cable channel known to man. She thought ruefully that just because she had been nursing a wounded heart all this time, she'd had no reason to think the others were all as happy with celibacy as she was.

She arched an eyebrow, wishing she hadn't spent so much time being nearly oblivious to the feelings of others.

"So…how was your evening at Date Tournament?"

"Scary. Sad," Laurie said dryly. "Want to hear about it?"

"Yes, but I want to get away from here first," Alex said. She could see across the lagoon, and the Tiki Hut was beginning to fill up for cocktail hour. Fishing parties returning, those who'd been out on scuba and snorkeling trips coming in, and those who had lazed the day away at the beach or the pool. She could see that Hank Adamson was talking to her boss, Jay Galway, head of operations at Moon Bay, and he was pointing toward the dolphin lagoons.

She didn't want to smile anymore, or suck up to Adamson—or defend herself. They were also standing with a man named Seth Granger, a frequent visitor, a very rich retired businessman who had decided he wanted to become a salvage expert. He signed up for dives and swims, then complained that they weren't adventurous enough. Alex had wished for a very long time that she could tell him not to go on the dives when he didn't enjoy the beauty of the reefs. Their dives were planned to show off the incredible color and beauty to be found on the only continental reef in the United States, not for a possible clash with modern-day pirates. Nor were they seeking treasure.

Well, if he wanted to talk about salvage or adventure, he could pin David down one night. They deserved each other.

Jay Galway seemed to be trying to get her attention. She pretended she didn't notice.

"Let's go to the beach on the other side of the island, huh? Then you can tell me all about dating hell," she said to Laurie.

"Mr. Galway is waving at you," Laurie said, running to catch up as Alex took off down the beach. "I think he wants you."

"Then move faster," Alex told her.

She turned, pretended she thought that James was just waving, waved back and took off at a walk so brisk it was nearly a run.

The dolphin lagoons were just around the bend, putting them on the westward side of the island rather than on the strip that faced the Atlantic. There were no roads out here from what wasn't even really the mainland, since they sat eastward of the Middle Keys. A motorboat regularly made the trip from the island to several of the Keys in about twenty minutes, and a small ferry traveled between several of the Keys, then stopped at the island, five times a day. Moon Bay had only existed for a few years; before it's purchase by a large German-American firm, it had been nothing more than a small strip of sand and trees where locals had come to picnic and find solitude.

The western side was still magnificently barren. White-sand beaches were edged by unbelievably clear water on one side, and palms and foliage on the other. Alex loved to escape the actual lodge area, especially at night. While their visitors were certainly free to roam in this direction, mercifully, not many did once it turned to the later portion of the afternoon. Sunbathers loved the area, but by now they were baked, red and in pain.

It was close to six, but the sun was still bright and warm. Nothing like the earlier hours, but nowhere near darkness. The water was calm and lazy; little nothing waves were creating a delicate foam against the shoreline that disappeared in seconds. The palms rustled behind them as they walked, and the delightful sea breeze kept the heat at bay.

Alex glanced up at the sky. It was a beautiful day, glorious. All kinds of tempests might be brewing out in the Atlantic or down in the Gulf somewhere, but here, all was calm and perfect. The sky was a rich, powdery blue, barely touched by the clouds, with that little bit of breeze deflecting the ninety-degree temperature that had slowly begun to drop.

Alex came to a halt and sat down on the wet sand. Laurie followed suit. The identical tank tops they wore—the words Moon Bay etched across black polyester in a soft off-white were light enough that Alex almost shivered when the breeze touched her damp arms. She had little concern for her matching shorts—they were made to take the sand, sun and heat with ease. It was comfortable clothing, perfect for the job, and not suggestive in the least. This was a family establishment.

A great place to run after a bad marriage, with everything she needed: a good job doing what she loved, water, boats, sand, sun, privacy.

Too much privacy.

And now…David was here. Damn him. She wasn't going to change a thing. She was going to do exactly what she had planned. Shower, dress nicely, blow-dry her hair, wear makeup…sip piña coladas and dance at the Tiki Hut. Flirt like hell with John Seymore. And ignore the fact that every single woman in the place would be eyeing David.

Over. It was over. They had gone their separate ways….

"Well?" Laurie said.

"I'm sorry. What?"

"Do you want to hear about Date Tournament? Or do you just want to sit here, me quietly at your side, while you damn yourself for divorcing such a hunk?"

"Never," Alex protested.

"Never as in, you never want to hear about Date Tournament, or never as in…what, exactly? You are divorced, right?"

"Of course. I meant, I'll never regret what I did. It was necessary."

"Why?"

Alex was silent. Why? We were going different ways? We didn't know one another to begin with? It was as simple as…Alicia Farr? No, that was ridiculous. It was complex, as most such matters were. It was his needing adventure at all costs, her needing to be a real trainer. It was…

"Oh my God!" Laurie gasped suddenly, staring at her. "Was he…he was abusive?"

"No! Don't be ridiculous."

"Then…?"

"We just went different ways."

"Hmph." Laurie toed a little crab back toward the water. "Whatever way he was going, I'd have followed him. But then, I've had the experience of Date Tournament, which you haven't—and which I thought you wanted to hear about."

"I'm sorry. I'm being a horrible friend. I'm in shock, I think. Having this lovely time with John Seymore, and then…up pops David."

"So what?"

"It's uncomfortable."

"But you and David are divorced, so what are you worried about? Enjoy John Seymore. He's a hunk, too. Not like anyone I met at Date Tournament."

"There must have been some nice guys."

"If there were, I didn't happen to meet them. Now let's get back to your love triangle."

Alex grinned. "There is no love triangle. Let's get back to you. You're gorgeous, bright, sweet and intelligent. The right guy is going to come along."

"Doesn't seem to be too much wrong with Mr. John Seymore. Did you know he's an ex-navy SEAL? But there you go. Apparently, when my right guy comes along, he wants to date you."

Alex arched an eyebrow, surprised. "I hadn't realized that…that…"

"You hadn't realized 'that' because there was no 'that' to realize. I hadn't even talked to the guy until today. Then there's your ex-husband."

"He's certainly a free agent."

"He's your ex. That's a no-no."

"I repeat—he's a free agent."

"One who sends you into a spiral," Laurie noted.

"I'm not in a spiral. It's just that…I was married to him. That makes me…I don't know what that makes me. Yes, I do. It makes me uncomfortable."

"You never fell out of love with him."

"Trust me—I did. It's just that…"

"All you've had for company since your divorce has been a bunch of sea animals?" Laurie suggested, amused.

"Neither one of us has dated in…a very, very long time," Alex agreed.

Laurie sighed glumly, setting her hands on her knees and cupping her chin in them. "Think it might be due to the fact that we've chosen to live on a remote island where the tourists are usually married, and the staff are usually in college?"

Alex laughed. "Maybe, but you'd think…sun, boats, island—fishing. Oh, well."

"What do you mean, oh well? At least there's excitement in your life. You've got the triangle thing going. Husband, lover."

"Ex-husband and new acquaintance," Alex reminded her.

"Ex-husband, new almost-lover. Vying for the same woman. And you know guys. They get into a competition thing. What a setup for jealousy and…"

Her voice trailed off, and she stared wide-eyed at Alex, like a doe in the headlights.

"Oh my God!" Laurie gasped.

She stared at Alex in pure horror. Alex frowned. "What? Come on, Laurie. Believe me, it's not that serious. You think that they'll get into some kind of a fight? No, never. In our marriage…David just didn't notice. Didn't care. I can't begin to see him decking someone—and sure as hell not over me."

"Oh my God," Laurie breathed again.

"Laurie, it's all right. Nothing is going to happen between David and John."

Laurie shook her head vehemently and slowly got to her feet, pointing. “Oh God, Alex. Look!”

For a moment, Alex couldn’t quite shift mental gears. Then she frowned, standing up herself.

“What?” she said to Laurie. She grasped her friend’s shoulders. “Laurie, what in the world is it?”

Laurie pointed. Alex realized that Laurie hadn’t been staring at her at all during the last few moments—she had been staring past her.

She spun around.

And that was when she saw the body on the beach.

Chapter 2

"I've read about you," John Seymore told David. "In the scuba magazines. That article on your work with great whites…wow. I've got to admit, I'm astounded to see you here. This place must seem pretty tame to you. It's great to get to meet you."

"Thanks," David said.

Seymore seemed pleasant. He was good-looking, well-muscled probably naturally, since he'd said he hadn't been out of military service long. Despite his surfer-boy blond hair and easy smile, there was a rough edge about him that betrayed age, maybe, and a hard life. David had a feeling his military stories would be the kind to make the hair rise on the back of the neck. Just as he had a feeling that, no matter how pleasant the guy might seem, he had a backbone of steel.

They'd started talking during the swim, and when Seymore had suggested a quick drink at the Tiki Hut, David had been glad to comply. He was interested in what would bring a man of John Seymore's expertise to such a charming little tourist haven.

"I know the people here," David told John. "The guy managing the place, Jay Galway, is a part-time thrill seeker. He's been on a few of my excursions over the years. I like coming here, but this is the first time I've stayed. The cottages are great. A perfect place to chill, with all the comforts of home, but you feel as if you're off somewhere in the wilds. What about you?"

"I know the water pretty well, but I've never had any fun with it. I've been out on the West Coast. I left the military…and, I'm afraid, a painful divorce."

"So you retired from the military," David said. "Living a life of ease, huh?"

Seymore laughed. "I did pretty well with the military, but not well enough to retire the way I'd like to. But my time is my own. I'm doing consulting work now. Because of my work in the service, I made some good contacts. But I needed a break, so I found this place on the Web. Seemed ideal, and so far, it has been."

Seymore was leaning on the bar, looking across the lagoon. Everyone was gone, but Seymore was staring as if someone was still there. Someone with features so delicately and perfectly proportioned that she was beautiful when totally drenched, devoid of all makeup, her hair showing touches of its radiant color despite the fact that it was heavy with sea water.

Despite himself, he felt a rise of something he didn't

like. Anger. Jealousy. And an age-old instinct to protect what was his. Except that she wasn't his anymore.

He had no rights here, and when he had first seen Alex this morning, after the initial shock in her eyes had died away, they had been narrowed and hostile each time they had fallen on him.

He lowered his head for a moment. You were the one who filed the papers, sweetie. Not a word to me, just a legal document.

I didn't come here because of you, he thought.

Okay, that was a lie. There had been no way he wouldn't show once Alicia's message had whetted his curiosity. He had come expecting to find Alicia Farr, even though, after he had returned her call and not heard back, warning signals had sounded in his mind. He wasn't surprised that she wasn't here, but he was worried.

And now he was feeling that age-old protective-instinct thing coming to the fore with Alex again—whether he did or didn't have the right to feel it. He told himself it was only because he was already on edge over Alicia. And anyway, maybe nothing was going on here. Maybe Alicia had made other arrangements and gone off on her own.

Or maybe someone was dead because of something going on here.

Unease filled him again.

Whatever had happened between Alex and him, the good and the bad, he couldn't help the tension he was feeling now. Especially where his wife was concerned. Ex-wife, he reminded himself. He wondered if he would ever accept that. Wondered if he would ever look at her and not believe they were still one.

Ever fall out of love with her.

Impatience ripped through him. He hated fools who went through life pining after someone who didn't want them in return. He hadn't pined. His life hadn't allowed for it.

That didn't mean that she didn't haunt his days, or that he didn't lie awake at night wondering why. Or that he didn't see her and feel that he would go after any guy who got near her. Or that he didn't see her, watch her move, see her enigmatic sea blue-green eyes, and want to demand to know what could have been so wrong that she had pushed him away.

All that was beside the point now. Yes, he had come here to meet Alicia. But he had come to meet Alicia because of Alex.

And now he was going to find out what was going on. Alex, of course, would believe that he was here only to find Alicia, to share in whatever find she had made. In her mind, he would be after the treasure, whatever that might be. Wanting the adventure, the leap into the unknown. No, she would never believe his main reason for being here was her, to watch over her, not when the danger wasn't solid, visible….

"Well," David murmured, swallowing a long draft of beer before continuing. "So you had a bad breakup, huh? They say you've got to be careful after a bad divorce. You know, watch out for rushing into things."

"Yeah, well," John told him, a half grin curving his lips, "they also say you've got to get right back on the horse after you fall off. Besides, I've been divorced about a year. You?"

"The same. About a year."

John Seymore studied him, that wry, half smile still in place. "I admit it. That's half the reason I wanted to buy you a drink. I know you were married to our dolphin instructor. Her name and picture were in one of the articles I read. I guess I wanted to make sure I wasn't horning in on a family reunion."

David could feel his jaw clenching. Screw Seymore. Being decent. Man, he hated that. He leaned on the counter, as well, staring out across the lagoon. "We split up a year ago," he said simply. "Alex is her own person."

What the hell else could he say? It was the truth. He could only hope his bitterness wasn't evident. Yet, even as the words were out of his mouth, he felt uneasy. He was, admittedly, distrustful of everyone right now, but this guy was suspicious of him, too. Here was an ex–navy SEAL, a man who knew more about diving than almost anyone else out there, at a resort where the facilities were great for tourists, but…a man with his experience?

A thought struck him, and he smiled. He was an honest man, but maybe this wasn't the time for the truth.

"Well," he said, "as far as she knows, she is, anyway."

"What does that mean?" Seymore asked him.

David waved a hand dismissively. "That's one of the reasons I'm here. There's a little technicality with our divorce. I wanted to let her know, find a convenient time for us to get together with an attorney, straighten it all out. But, hey…" He clapped a hand on Seymore's shoulder. "It's fine. Really. I think I'll go take a long hot shower. I'm beginning to feel a little salt encrusted. Thanks for the beer."

Seymore nodded, looking a little troubled. "Yeah, I…I guess I'll go hit the shower, too."

"My treat next go-around," David said. Then he set down his glass, turned, and left the Tiki Hut.

It was definitely a body. Alex and Laurie could both clearly see that, despite the seaweed clinging to it.

Alex started to rush forward, but Laurie grabbed her arm. "Wait! If she's dead, and you touch her, we could destroy forensic evidence."

"You've been watching too much TV," Alex threw over her shoulder as she pulled free.

But she came to a halt a few feet from the body. The stench was almost overwhelming. It was a woman, but she couldn't possibly be alive. Alex could see a trail of long blond hair tangled around the face.

She had to be sure.

Turning, taking a deep breath and holding it, Alex stepped forward and hunched down by the woman. She extended a hand to the throat, seeking a pulse. A crab crawled out of the mound of seaweed and hair, causing her to cry out.

"What?" Laurie shouted.

"Crab," Alex replied quickly. Bile rumbled in her stomach, raced toward her throat. She gritted her teeth, swallowed hard and felt the icy coldness of the woman's flesh. No pulse. The woman was dead. Alex rose, hurrying back to Laurie.

"She's dead. I'll stay here, you go for help."

"I'm not leaving you here alone with a corpse."

"Okay, you stay, I'll go."

"You're not leaving me here alone with a corpse!"

"Laurie—"

"She's dead. She's not going anywhere. We'll both go for help."

"Yes, but what if someone…what if a child comes out here while we're gone?"

"What?" Laurie demanded. "You think I'm going to throw myself on top of a corpse to hide it? There's nothing we can do except hurry."

"I'm not afraid to be alone with a corpse."

"You should be. What if the person who turned her into a corpse is still around here somewhere?"

Alex felt an uneasy sensation, but it was ridiculous. She shook her head. "Laurie, she's drifted in from… from somewhere else. She's been in the water a while."

"Maybe. Neither one of us is an expert."

"Laurie, that…stink takes a while to occur."

"Let's just hurry. We won't be long, and she won't go anywhere."

"All right, then, let's go."

They tore back along the path they had taken and minutes later, neared the Tiki Hut. Laurie opened her mouth, ready to shout.

Alex clamped her hand over it. "No!"

Laurie fought free. "Alex! Did you touch that corpse with that hand? Maybe she died of some disease."

Alex had to admit she hadn't thought of such a possibility. She winced, but said, "We can't just start shouting about a corpse. We'll cause a panic."

She scanned the Tiki Hut. The mothers who had been on the swim earlier were there—the teens were evidently off somewhere else. She would have liked to see

John Seymore. Since he was an ex–navy SEAL, he would surely know how to handle the situation.

She would even have liked to see David, Mr. Competence himself. Cool, collected, a well of strength in handling any given situation.

"Let's find Jay," she said.

She caught Laurie by the elbow, leading her past the Tiki Hut and along the flower-bordered stone pathway that led to the lobby of the lodge. They burst in, rushing to the desk. Luckily, no one was checking in or out. Len Creighton was on duty. Thirtyish, slim, pleasant, he smiled as he saw them, and then he saw their panic and his smile faded.

"Len, I need Jay. Where is he?"

Len cast a glance over his shoulder, indicating the inner office.

She headed straight back.

Jay wasn't there.

"He's not here," she called.

"I'll page him."

His voice was smooth as silk, hardly creating a blip against the soft music that always played in the lobby.

Moments later, Jay Galway, looking only slightly irritated, came striding across the lobby.

He was tall and lean, with sleek, dark hair, expressive gray eyes and a thin, aesthetic face. Patrician nose. His lips were a bit narrow, but they added to the look almost of royalty that he carried like an aura about him. She really liked her boss. They were friends, and he had always been ready to support her in her decisions, even if he didn't agree with them. She'd known him before she'd come to work here. In fact, he'd called her about the job when he'd heard about the divorce.

He paused in front of the counter, perfect in an Armani suit, and stared at her questioningly.

"What on earth is this all about?" he demanded.

He was still a short distance away from her, and a few guests had just come in and were heading in their direction.

"I need to talk to you. Alone." She glanced meaningfully at Len.

"I hide nothing from Len."

Alex glanced at Len and wondered if there was more going on between the two men than she knew. Not that she cared, or had time to worry about it now.

"There's a body on the beach," she said very softly.

"A body," echoed Laurie, who was standing behind her.

He stared at her as if she had lost her mind. "This is Florida, honey. There are a lot of bodies on the beach."

Alex groaned inwardly. "A dead body, Jay."

"A dead body?" Len exclaimed loudly.

They all stared at him. "Sorry," he said quickly.

Jay gave his full attention to her at last, staring at her hard, his eyes narrowing. His focus never left her face, but he warned Len, "Shut up. I mean it. That reporter is around somewhere. All we need is him getting his nose into this."

Alex stared back at him, aghast. "Someone is dead, Jay. It's not a matter of worrying about publicity. Will you call the sheriff's office—please?"

"Right. Len, call the county boys and ask them to send someone out. Someone from homicide."

"Homicide?" Laurie murmured. "Maybe she just…drowned."

"It still needs to be investigated," Alex said, still staring at Jay. His behavior puzzled her. They had no idea who the dead woman might be, where she had come from, or even if there was a murderer loose in paradise, and he seemed so blasé.

Finally he said, "Show me."

"Let's go."

Len started to follow, but Jay spun on him. "You're on duty. And you," Jay warned Alex, "make it look as if we're taking a casual stroll."

"Jay, honestly, sometimes—"

"Alex, want to cause a panic?" Jay demanded.

"Sure. Fine. We're taking a casual stroll."

They left the lobby, Alex leading, Jay behind her, Laurie following quickly. They took the path through the flowers, passed the Tiki Hut—which seemed unusually quiet for the time of day—and around the lagoon area.

"Alex, slow down. We're taking a stroll, remember?" Jay said.

She looked back, still moving quickly. "Jay, we're in shorts and you're in an Armani suit, about to get sand in your polished black shoes. How casually can we stroll?"

He let out a sound of irritation but argued the point no further.

They reached the pristine sand beach. The temperature was dropping, the sweet breeze still blowing in.

Alex came to a halt. Jay nearly crashed into her back. As if they were a vaudeville act, Laurie collided with him.

"What the hell?" Jay demanded.

"It's gone," Alex breathed.

"What's gone?" Jay demanded.

"The body."

Laurie was staring toward the thatch of seaweed where the corpse had lain. She, too, seemed incredulous. "It—it is gone," she murmured.

Without turning, Alex could feel the way that Jay was looking at her. Like an icy blast against the balmy summer breeze, she could feel his eyes boring into her back.

She didn't turn but ran down the length of the beach, searching the sand and the water, looking for any hint as to where the body had been moved.

"What, Alex?" Jay shouted. "You saw a corpse, but it rolled down the beach to catch the sun better?"

She stopped then, whirling around.

"It's moved," she said, walking back to where Jay stood.

"Your corpse got up and walked?"

She exhaled impatiently. "Jay, it was here."

"Really, Jay, it was," Laurie said, coming to her defense.

They all turned at the sound of a motor. A sheriff's department launch was heading their way. Nigel Thompson, the sheriff himself, had come.

Usually Alex liked Nigel Thompson. He looked just the way she figured an old-time Southern sheriff should look. He was somewhere between fifty and sixty years old; his eyes were pale blue, his hair snow-white. He was tall and heavy, a big man. His appearance was customarily reassuring.

He tended to be a skeptic.

A skeptic when rowdy, underage kids told their stories. A skeptic when adults who should have known better lied about the amount they had been drinking before a boating accident. He was never impolite, never skirted the law, but he was tough, and folks around here knew it.

He cut the motor but drew his launch right up to the beach. Hopping from the craft, he demanded, "Where's this body?"

Jay looked from Nigel to Alex.

"Well?" he asked her.

She lifted her chin, grinding down hard on her teeth. She looked at Nigel. "It was right here," she said pointing.

He looked from the sand and seaweed to her. "It was there?"

"I swear to you, it was right there."

He looked at Alex, slowly arching an eyebrow. "Alexandra, I was just about to sit down to dinner when the call came in. Tell me this isn't a joke or a summer prank."

"Had to have been a prank—and Alex fell for it," Jay said. He didn't sound angry with her, but he did sound aggravated.

"I'm here now," Nigel said, looking at Alex. "So tell me what you saw."

"A sunbather who thought it was one hell of a joke to fool someone into thinking she was dead," Jay said.

"She was dead," Alex said. "Nigel, you've known me for years. Do I make things up?"

"No, missy, you don't," the sheriff acknowledged. "But there is no body," he pointed out.

"It was here, right here. I got close enough to make sure she was...I touched her. She was dead," Alex asserted with quiet vehemence.

"She sure looked dead," Laurie offered.

Alex winced inwardly, aware her friend was trying

to help. But her words gave the entire situation an aura of doubt.

"She was dead," Alex repeated.

"Cause of death?" Nigel asked her.

"I didn't do an autopsy," she snapped, and then was furious with herself.

"There was nothing that suggested a cause of death?" Nigel asked patiently.

She shook her head. "If she had washed up with a rope around her neck, I didn't see it. I'm sorry, I've dealt with dead dolphins, but I never interned at the morgue," Alex told him. "But I know a corpse when I see one."

"So you've seen lots of corpses?" Jay asked.

"I've seen enough dead mammals, Jay." She looked at Nigel. "I swear to you that there was a dead woman here, tangled in seaweed."

He sighed, looking at the sand and the water, then back to her. "No drag marks, Alex. She wasn't pulled into the bushes."

"She was here," Alex insisted stubbornly.

"Alex, I'm not saying this is what happened, but isn't it possible that someone was pulling a prank?"

"No," she said determinedly.

"So…what did happen? Why isn't she here?"

"I don't know. I thought she was far enough out of the water, so I don't think the waves could have pulled her back out… I think someone came and moved her."

"They were quick," Nigel commented.

"I'm telling you, she was here. Isn't there a way you can check? It will be dark soon. Can't you spray something around, see if there are specks of blood in the seaweed or on the sand anywhere? Better yet, take samples.

Get more men out here and make certain that the only tracks around came from Jay, Laurie and myself?"

"There could be dozens of tracks around, and it wouldn't mean anything. The beach is accessible to all the staff and every guest," Nigel told her.

"Surely there's something you can do," Alex said.

"I can see if a body turns up again," he told her quietly. "Seriously, Alex. The most likely scenario is that the woman wasn't dead. Maybe she was unconscious but came to while you were up at the lodge. One of you should have stayed here."

Alex glared at Laurie.

Laurie looked back at her defensively. "Hey, how could I know that a corpse could get up and walk away?"

"A corpse can't get up and walk away," Jay interjected impatiently. "Unless the person you saw was not a corpse."

"We're going in circles here," Alex told him.

"This is ridiculous," he told her. "You pull me out here, make me ruin my good Italian shoes, drag Nigel away from his supper…because you saw someone passed out. Maybe someone in need of help, who you left. Or, more likely, someone playing a joke. A sick joke, yes. But a joke, and you fell for it."

Alex lifted her hands in exasperation. "All right, fine. There's nothing I can say or do to make you believe me. Nigel, I'm sorry about your supper. I owe you one. I'm going to take a shower."

"Wait a minute," Nigel said. "I'm not ignoring this. I'll make a check on passengers who took the ferry over today, and, Jay, you check your guest lists. We'll make sure that everyone is accounted for."

Alex stood in stony silence.

"Alex, that's all I can do since there's no body," Nigel said patiently. "We're not New York, D.C., or even Miami. I don't have a huge forensic department or the manpower to start combing every strand of seaweed, especially since the tide is coming in. Alex, please. I'm not mocking you. It's just that there is no body." He turned to Jay. "Get busy on the paperwork, Jay. I'll handle the ferry records. And, Alex…don't mention this around, all right?"

She frowned curiously at him. "But—"

"Don't you dare go alarming the guests with a wild story," Jay said.

"Actually, I was thinking that if there was a corpse and someone's hidden it, it might be a very dangerous topic of conversation," Nigel told her.

"He's right," Jay said. He pointed a finger toward Alex. "No mention of this. No mention of it for your own safety."

"Oh, yeah, right."

Nigel turned around, looking at the beach. He shook his head and started away.

"Where you going, Nigel?" Jay asked.

"To check on the ferry records," Nigel called back.

He reached his launch, gave it a shove back to the water and waded around to hop in, then gave them a wave.

Jay stared at Alex and Laurie again. "Not a word, you understand? Not a word. It doesn't matter if there were a dozen corpses on the beach, Alex, they're not here now. So keep quiet."

"Fine. Not a word, Jay," Alex snapped, walking past him.

"Hey! I'm your boss, remember?" he told her.

She kept walking, Laurie following in her tracks.

"I'm still your boss," he called after her. "And you owe me a new pair of shoes."

They were soon out of earshot. "Alex, there really was a corpse, wasn't there?" Laurie asked. But she sounded uncertain.

"Yes."

"Perhaps...I mean...couldn't you have been mistaken?"

"No." She turned. "I'm going to go take a hot shower and a couple of aspirin. I'll see you later."

Laurie nodded, still looking uncertain. "I'm sorry. Jay has a way of twisting things," Laurie said apologetically.

"I know. Forget it. I'll see you later."

She lifted a hand and turned down a slender trail that led through small palms and hibiscus, anxious only to reach her little cottage.

She slid her plastic key from the button pocket of her uniform shorts and inserted it into the lock. The door swung open.

The air was on; the ceiling fan in the whitewashed and rattan-furnished living-room area was whirling away. The coolness struck her pleasantly.

She walked through the living area and into the small kitchen, pausing to pull a wine cooler from the refrigerator. She uncapped it quickly and moved on, anxious to flop down on the sofa out on the porch. She opened the floor-to-ceiling glass doors and went out, actually glad of the wave of warmth outside, tempered by the feel of the night breeze and the hypnotic whirl of another ceiling fan.

But even as she fell into a chair, she tensed, sitting straight up and staring across to the charming white gingerbread railing, too startled by a figure looming in the shadows of coming twilight to scream. Then she took a deep breath of relief when she recognized who it was.

It wasn't just anyone planted on her porch.

It was David.

He was wearing nothing but swim trunks, broad, bronzed shoulders gleaming, arms crossed over his chest as he leaned against the rail. He was very still, and yet, as it had always been with him, it seemed that he emanated energy, as if any moment he would move like a streak of lightning.

Her heart lurched. He was so familiar. How many times had she seen him like this and walked up to him, wherever they were, sliding her fingers down his naked back, sometimes feeling the heat of the sun and sometimes just that of the man? She had loved the way he had turned to her in response and taken her into the curl of his arm.

How many times had it led to so much more? There had been those days when, just in from the water, he had been speaking to a TV camera, holding her as he talked, then had suddenly turned to her, and she had seen a sudden light rise in his eyes. She could remember the way he would move, his attention only for her, as he excused himself, smiled and led her away. By the time they reached a private spot, they would both be breathless, laughing and pulling at the few pieces of clothing they were wearing. He could move with such languid, sinewy power; the tone of his voice could change so easily; the lightest brush of his fingers could evoke a thousand rays of pure sensuality. And she had been so desperately, insanely eager to know them all.

But then, that had been in the days when it had mattered to him that she was with him.

He didn't smile now. His deep blue eyes were grave as he surveyed her. She'd seen him cold and distant like this, as well, the light in his eyes almost predatory.

"David," she said dryly, pushing away the past, forcing herself to forget the intimacy and remember only what it had been like once she had determined to pursue her own career and he had begun to travel without her. Days, weeks, even a month…gone. Not even a telephone call, once he was with his true love. The sea.

And those who traveled it with him.

"Alex," he responded. "I've been waiting for you."

"So it appears. Well, how nice to see you. Here. On my porch. My personal porch, my private space. Gee, this is great." Her tone couldn't have held more acidity.

"Thanks." Her welcome hadn't been sincere. Neither was his gratitude. But there was no mistaking the seriousness of his next words.

"So," he said, "tell me about the body you found—the one that disappeared from the beach."

Chapter 3

"What?" she said sharply.

"You heard me. Tell me about the body." He uncoiled from his position, coming toward her, taking a chair near hers. He was close, too close, and she instantly felt wary and, despite herself, unnerved. They'd been apart for a year, and she still felt far too familiar with the rugged planes of his face, the bronzed contours of his hands and fingers, idly folded now before him.

She managed to sit back, eyeing him with dignity and, she hoped, a certain disdain.

"What the hell are you doing on my porch? There's a lobby for guests."

"Get off it. You must have been in a panic. And Jay probably behaved like an asshole."

"I don't know what you're talking about."

"I'm trying to help you out."

"If you want to help me out, get off the island."

"Am I making you uneasy?"

"You bet," she told him flatly.

That drew a smile to his lips. "Missed me, huh?"

She sat farther forward, setting her wine cooler on the rattan coffee table, preparing to rise.

"I assume you have a room. Why don't you go put some clothes on."

"Ah, that's it. Can't take the sight of my naked chest. It's making you hot, huh?"

"More like leaving me cold," she said icily. "Now go away, please."

His smile faded for a moment. "Don't worry. I know you want me to leave. I haven't forgotten that you had the divorce papers sent to me without a word."

"What was left to say?" she asked with what she hoped was quiet dignity.

"Hmm, let me think. Maybe your reasons for leaving me?"

She got to her feet. "You want the truth? I couldn't take it. I was so in love with you, it hurt all the time. You were all that mattered to me. My dolphins were far too tame for you—and far too unimportant. Our agreement that we'd spend time dedicated to my pursuits didn't mean a thing—not if a sunken ship turned up or a shark-research expedition was formed. Then it came to the point when I said you were welcome to go off even when you were supposed to be helping me—and you went. And then that became a way of life. There's the story in a nutshell. You were gone long before I sent those papers. And sometime in there, I got over you. I love working with dolphins. No, it isn't like finding a Spanish galleon, or even locating a yacht that went down ten years ago, maybe. But I love it. What you apparently needed, or wanted, was a different kind of wife. Either a pretty airhead who would follow you endlessly, or…someone as fanatic about treasure as you are. So go to your room and put some clothes on, or take a stroll over to the Tiki Hut and give someone else a thrill."

She started inside, hoping he would stop her. Not because she wanted to be near him, but because he knew about the body.

Her back to him, she suddenly wondered how he knew. The question left her with a very uneasy feeling.

"Alexandra, whatever anger you're feeling toward me, whatever I did or didn't do, I swear, I'm just trying to help you now."

She spun around. "How do you know about the body, anyway? Jay gave me very direct orders not to mention it to anyone."

He cocked his head slightly. "Jay's assistant talks."

"What did you do? Flirt with Len, too?"

He arched an eyebrow, curiously, slowly. She wished she could take back the comment. It made it appear as if…as if jealousy had been the driving factor in her quest for freedom. And it hadn't been.

Thankfully, David didn't follow up on her comment. "I don't think Len could contain himself. He tried to be smooth and cool, but I guess he feels he knows me and that I'm intelligent enough not to repeat what he said. He told me you'd all gone off in search of a body, and then it turned out to be gone. I overheard Jay tell him that part."

She stood very still, watching him for a long moment. "You know, I came back here to be alone."

"So talk to me, then I'll leave you alone."

"You know, this is very strange. Most people would scoff at the idea immediately. Bodies don't turn up on a daily basis. And yet…it sounds as if you think that there…should have been a body."

"No," he corrected. "I didn't say I thought there should be a body."

Alex pressed her fingers to her temples. "I can't do this," she said.

She was startled when he suddenly moved close to her. "Alex, please. If there was a body, and you saw it—you could be in danger."

She sighed. "Not if no one knows about the body."

"But I know, so others could, as well."

"You said Len only told you about it because he trusts you."

"Others might have overheard."

"Just what do you want?"

He was no more than an inch from her. He still carried the scent of salt and the sea, and it was a compelling mixture. She looked away.

"I don't want anything. I'm deeply concerned. Alex, don't you understand? You could be in danger!" His hands fell on her shoulders then. It was suddenly like old times. "You have to listen to me."

She'd heard the words before. Felt his hands before. Memories of being crushed against that chest stirred within her. She didn't want to believe that she had once been so in love with him just because he was so distinctively male and sensual. There had been times when they were together when his smile had been so quick, and then so lazy, when just a finger trailing across her bare arm or shoulder had…

"David, let go of me," she said, stepping back.

His eyes were narrowed, hard. She'd seen them that way before, when he was intent on getting to the bottom of something.

"Talk to me, Alex."

"All right. Yes, Jay acted like an asshole. Yes, I'm convinced I saw a body. A woman. A blonde. Other than that…I couldn't see her face. The angle of her body was wrong, and she was tangled in seaweed. When we went back, she was gone. Even Laurie, who saw the body first, wasn't sure we'd seen it anymore. She didn't actually go near the body even when it was there. Anyway, there was no corpse. So, are you happy?"

He didn't look happy. Actually, for a moment, he appeared ashen. She wanted to touch his face, but he was still David. Solid as rock.

"Please, will you leave me alone?" she asked him.

His voice was strange, scratchy, when he spoke. "I can't leave you alone. Not now," he said. And yet, contrary to his words, he turned and left her porch, disappearing along the back trail that led, in a roundabout way, to the other cottages and the lodge.

She stared after him, suddenly feeling the overwhelming urge to burst into tears. "Damn it, I got over you," she grated out. "And here you are again, driving me crazy, making me doubt myself…and not doubt myself," she finished softly.

She realized suddenly that twilight was coming.

And that she was afraid.

David had almost made her forget. No matter what anyone said, she'd seen a body on the beach. That was shattering in itself, but then the body had disappeared.

She slipped back inside, locking the sliding-glass door behind her. Then she looked outside and saw the shadows of dusk stretching out across the landscape.

She drew the curtains, uneasily checked her front door, and at last—after opening and finishing a new wine cooler—she managed to convince herself to take a shower.

David sat at a table at the Tiki Hut, watching Alex. Not happily. He had been sitting with Jay Galway, who hadn't mentioned Alex's discovery, naturally. There might be a major exodus from the lodge if word got out that a mysterious body had been found, then disappeared, and Galway would never stand for that.

During their conversation, David had asked Jay casually about recent guests, and any news in the world of salvage or the sea, and Jay had been just as cool, shrugging, and saying that, with summer in full swing, most of their guests were tourists, eager to swim with the dolphins, or snorkel or dive on the Florida reef. Naturally—that was what they were set up to do.

David had showered, changed and made a few phone calls in the time since he'd left Alex. He'd still arrived before her.

If she'd seen him at the table, she'd given him no notice, heading straight for the table where John Seymore was sitting with Hank Adamson. They were chatting now, and he had the feeling that part of Alex's bubbling enthusiasm and the little intimate touches she was giving Seymore were strictly for his benefit, her message clear: Leave me the hell alone, hands off, I've moved on.

How far would it go?

All right, one way or the other, he would have been jealous, but now he was really concerned.

A woman's body had been found on the beach, and he had not heard back from Alicia Farr—who was a blonde.

David couldn't stop the reel playing through his head.

From what he'd overheard, Jay was convinced a trick had been played, or that Alex had assumed a dozing sunbather was a corpse. David didn't see that as a possibility. Alex was far too intelligent, and she wouldn't have walked away without assuring herself that the body no longer maintained the least semblance of a vital sign.

A trick? Maybe.

Real corpses didn't get up and walk away, but they could be moved.

If there had been a real corpse and it had been moved, it had been moved by someone on the island. That meant Alex could be in serious danger. After all, Len had told David what was going on, so who knew who else he might have told?

An ex–navy SEAL, maybe? The perfect blond hero—but was that the truth behind John Seymore being at Moon Bay?

Hopefully he would find out soon enough.

"So?"

"I'm sorry, what did you say?" David said, realizing that Jay had been talking away, but he hadn't heard a word.

"Well? Is it a photojournalism thing or a salvage dive?"

"What…?"

"Your next excursion," Jay said.

"Oh...well, I was looking into something, but my source seems to have dried up," David told Jay. My key source either dried up, or was killed and washed up on your beach, and then disappeared, he thought. Then his attention was caught by Alex again.

The band was playing a rumba. She was up and in John Seymore's arms. Head cast back, she was laughing at whatever he had to say. Her eyes were like gems. She was beautifully decked out in heels and a soft yellow halter dress that emphasized both her tan and her tall, sinewy length. Her long hair was free and a true golden blond, almost surreal in the light of the torches that burned here by night.

The lights were actually bug repellents. There was no escaping the fact that when you had foliage like this, you had bugs. But the glow they gave everything, especially Alex, was almost hypnotic.

David turned to Jay. "Sure you haven't heard about anything?" he asked him.

"Me?" Galway laughed. "Hell, I'm a hanger-on. The big excitement in my life is when I get a taste of something because of the big-timers—like you."

"Well, I'm looking at the moment," David told him. "So, if you do get wind of anything, anything at all, I'd like to know."

"You'd be the first one I'd go to," Jay assured him solemnly.

"Interesting that you'd say so—with Seth Granger here and ready to pay." And in the Tiki Hut at that moment, David realized. Granger was a big man and in excellent shape for his sixty-odd years. He was speaking with Ally Conroy, mother of Zach, at the bar. She was at least twenty years his junior, but he'd gathered from their bits of conversation before the swim that she was a widow, worried about rearing her son alone. Seth wasn't all that well-liked by many people, yet Ally seemed to be giving him the admiration he craved. Maybe they were a perfect fit.

"Seth…well, you know. He's always looking for something to bug his way into. Hell, why not? He's rich, and he loves the sea, and he'd like to make a name for himself in his retirement years. Don't you love it? Tons of money, no real knowledge, yet he wants to be right in the thick of things. Executive turned explorer."

"Why not?" David said with a shrug. "Most expeditions need financial backing."

"Yeah, why not? It's what I'd love to do myself. I've got a great job here, mind you—but I sure wish I had his resources. Or your reputation. Every major corporation out there with a water-related product to sell is willing to finance you—even on a total wild-goose chase."

"You know me—game for anything that has to do with the water," David murmured absently.

Alex was leaning very close to John Seymore now. In a moment she'd be spilling out of her dress.

"Excuse me," he said to Jay, rising, then went up to the couple on the floor. Alex wouldn't be happy, but if John Seymore was really such an all-right kind of guy—or even pretending to be one—he would show him the courtesy of allowing him to cut in.

A tap on Seymore's shoulder assured him that he had correctly assessed the situation. The other man, his eyes full of confident good humor, stepped back.

Alex gave David a look of sheer venom. But she wasn't going to cause a scene in the Tiki Hut. She slipped into his arms.

"What are you doing?" she asked him.

"Dancing."

"You know I don't want to dance with you."

He ignored her and said, "I guess you haven't had a chance to talk with Seymore yet."

"John and I have done lots of talking."

"Well, I happened to mention to him one of the reasons I'm here."

"And it has something to do with me?"

"Definitely."

She arched a delicate eyebrow. "I guess you're going to tell me—whether I want to know or not."

"We're not divorced."

"Don't be ridiculous," she said sharply. "I filed papers, you signed them."

"I don't quite get it myself, but apparently there was some little legal flaw. I must not have signed on all the dotted lines. The documents were never properly filed, and therefore the decision was declared null and void. I know what a busy woman you are, but I need to ask you when would be a good time to get together with my lawyer and rectify the situation."

She wasn't even pretending to dance anymore. She just stood on the floor, staring at him. His arms were still around her, tendrils of silky soft, newly washed blond hair slipping over his hands, teasing in their sensuality. He knew he needed to move away, but he didn't.

"That's impossible!" she exclaimed.

"Sorry."

She stared at him, still amazed. "I don't...I... can't..."

"Look, Alex, I know how eager you are to be completely rid of me. I'm sorry. But as of this moment, we are still married."

He wondered if lightning would come out of the sky to strike him dead.

It didn't.

God must have understood his situation.

"It's...it's impossible," she repeated.

He shrugged, as if in complete understanding of her dismay. "I'm sorry."

Something hardened in the depths of her ever-changing, sea-green eyes. "I'll make time to see your attorney."

"Great. We'll set it up. Well, lover boy is waiting, so I'll let you go in a sec. But first I need you to listen to me. Alex, I'm begging you, listen to me. You've got to be careful."

She pulled back, searching his eyes, then shaking her head. "David, I understand why you're here, and frankly, I'm surprised you took the time to actually ask me what would be convenient for me. But I don't quite get this sudden interest. Where's Bebe whats-her-name? Or the thin-but-oh-so-stacked Alicia Farr, the Harvard scholar?"

Her question sent an eerie chill up his spine. *I think she's your disappearing body.*

"Alex, I'm afraid you're in danger." His words, he realized, sounded stiff and cold.

She shook her head. "No one else believes I discovered a corpse. Why should you?"

He hesitated for a minute. "I know you," he told her.

"You're not a fool. You would have looked closely enough to know."

"Well, thanks for the compliment. I wish Nigel Thompson felt that way. I couldn't get through to him that though it's improbable that a body was really there and somehow moved, it's not impossible. So if you'll let me off the dance floor…?"

He released her. But as she started to step past him, he caught her arm. She looked up, and for a moment, her eyes were vulnerable. Her scent seemed to wrap around him, caress him.

"Don't trust anyone," he said.

"I certainly don't trust you."

He pulled her back around to face him. "You know what? I've about had it with this."

"Oh, you have, have you?"

"I got a long lecture. You can have one, too. You read a lot into a number of situations that just wasn't there. You never had the right not to trust me. It was just that, to you, the minute a phone or a radio didn't work, I had to be doing something. With someone. And you know what, Alex? That kind of thing gets really old, really quick."

"Sorry, but it's over anyway, isn't it? You received the divorce papers and said, 'Hey, go right ahead.' You were probably thankful you didn't have to deal with any annoying baggage anymore. And now you're suddenly going to be my champion, defending me from a danger that doesn't exist?"

"Alex, you know me. You know what kind of man I am. Hell, hate me 'til the sun falls from the sky, but trust me right now."

"There are dozens of people here. I don't think I'm in any danger in the middle of the Tiki Hut. And trust you?" She sounded angry, then a slow smile curved her lips.

"What?"

"I just find it rather amusing that you're suddenly so determined to enjoy my company. There were so many times when…well, never mind."

He stared at her blankly for a moment. "What are you talking about?"

"It doesn't matter anymore. It's over."

"Actually, it's not," he said. Again he waited for lightning to strike. Not that it should. He was doing this out of a very real fear for her life.

She waved a hand in the air. "All over but the shouting," she murmured.

"Maybe that's what we were lacking—the shouting."

"Great. We should have had a few more fights?"

It was strange, he thought, but this was almost a conversation, a real one.

And then John Seymore chose that exact moment to return, tapping him on the shoulder. "Since you're on the dance floor and not actually dancing…?"

"And it's a salsa," Alex put in.

"Salsa?" John murmured. "I'm not sure I know what I'm doing, but—"

"I do," David said quickly, grinning, and catching Alex in his arms once again. "I'll bring her back for the next number."

"Since when do you salsa?" Alex demanded as they began to move.

"Since a friend married a dance instructor," he told her.

She seemed startled, but he really did know what he

was doing. He'd never imagined the dance instruction he'd so recently received from a friend's wife would pay off so quickly. Alex was good, too. She'd probably honed her skills working here, being pleasant to the guests in the Tiki Hut at night.

After a minute, though, he wasn't quite sure what he had gained. They looked good together on the floor, and he knew it. But the music was fast, so conversation was impossible. At the end of the song he managed to lead her into a perfect dip, so at least he was rewarded by the amazement in her eyes as they met his.

In fact, she stayed in his arms for several extra seconds, staring up at him before realizing that the music had ended and the gathering in the Tiki Hut was applauding them.

He grinned slowly as she straightened, then pushed against his chest. "The dance is over," she said firmly, then walked quickly away.

"You really are a man of many talents."

Turning, he saw Alex's assistant, the pretty young blonde. She was leaning against the edge of the rustic wood bar.

"Thanks."

"Do you cha-cha?" she asked, smiling.

"Yes, I do," he said.

"Well, will you ask me? Or are you making me ask you?"

"Laurie, I would love to dance with you," he said gallantly.

As they moved, she asked him frankly, "Why on earth did you two ever split up?"

"Actually, I don't really know," he told her.

"I bet I do," she told him. "You must be pretty high maintenance."

"High maintenance? I'm great at taking care of myself. I may not be a gourmet, but I can cook. I know every button on a washing machine. I usually even remember to put down the toilet seat."

She laughed. "Well, there you go."

"Excuse me? How is that high maintenance?"

"You don't need anybody," she said. "So it's high maintenance for someone to figure out what they can do for you."

She wasn't making any sense, but she was sincere, and she made him smile.

Then the music came to an end, and he regretted that he had been so determined on proving his mettle with Alex, because he found himself being asked to dance by almost every woman in the Tiki Hut.

And somewhere, in the middle of a mambo, he realized that Alex had slipped away—and so had John Seymore.

Somehow, just when things had begun looking a little brighter, David had walked back into her life, and now he was ruining everything.

John's arm sat casually around her shoulders as they strolled toward her cottage. "Hate to admit it," he said casually, "but you two looked great out there. Did you spend a lot of time out dancing while you were married?"

"No. We didn't spend much time together doing anything—other than diving for treasure or facing great whites or experiencing some other thrill."

"Strange," he said.

"What?"

"The way you sound. You love the sea so much, too."

"Actually? I'm not into sharks. I was terrified every time I went into the water with them, but with the crew of hard-core fanatics that always seemed to be around, I didn't want to look like a coward. I love the sea, yes. But I'm into warm-blooded, friendly creatures, myself."

"You really love your dolphins, huh?"

She shrugged, liking the way his arm felt around her, but feeling a sense of discomfort, as well.

David. Telling her that they were still married. But they weren't; they hadn't been for a year. Not in any way that mattered. All he was talking about was legality. His words shouldn't mean a thing.

Except that…

She was traditional. She'd been raised Catholic.

Damn David. He would know her thought process, that she would feel that she shouldn't be with another man, that it wouldn't be right, and…

Just how many women had he been with in the last year? What was wrong with her that she couldn't see how ridiculous it was for her to be concerned over anything he had to say? Why had seeing him again made her uncertain, when she knew that an easy confidence and charm were just a part of his nature?

"I do love my dolphins," she said, realizing she had been silent for too long after his question. "They are the most incredible animals. What I like most is that they seem to study us just as we study them, and just as we learn their behavior, they learn what our behavior is going to be. Sometimes their affinity for man, especially in the wild, can be dangerous for them, but still, the communication we can share is just amazing."

"They are incredible," he agreed. "I've seen them used in the navy in the most remarkable ways. Never worked with them myself," he added quickly. "But I've seen what they can do."

They had reached her porch. Strange, her thoughts had been filled with David's behavior—she wished she could begin to understand the male of her own species half as well as she understood her dolphins—and then with John's company, which, she had to admit, she had found all the more intoxicating just because she knew that it disturbed David.

Now, despite the light burning on her back porch, it seemed that the shadows of night were all around her, and she remembered the body on the beach. It wasn't that she had ever forgotten, but despite her determination, the doubts of others had crept into her mind.

Was she insane, thinking the woman had been dead?

Or was she more insane now, trying to do what Jay had demanded, keep silent about the possibility of a body on the beach?

John had escorted her up the two wooden steps to her little back porch, with its charming, gingerbread railing. They were standing by her back door.

He was probably waiting to be invited in.

And just this morning, she had thought that if this moment came, she would invite him in.

She mentally damned her ex-husband again. Her almost-ex-husband.

She smiled up at John Seymore. His dimple was showing as he offered her a rueful smile.

"You're really something," he said.

"So are you," she murmured. Blond hair, handsome face, shoulders to die for, arms that were wonderfully secure…

She slipped into them. He lowered his mouth to hers, and she allowed herself the kiss, but she couldn't stop herself from analyzing it. Firm mouth, coercive, not demanding, fingers gently suggestive in her hair, tongue teasing at her lips, slipping into her mouth, warm, very warm, definitely seductive…

On a physical level, he was incredible.

So if she could just forget about David…

She couldn't. Not when he was here, on the island, so irritatingly in-her-face.

She stepped back, stroking John's cheek.

"You're around for a little while longer, right?" she inquired softly, hoping he understood her signals. I'm interested, but it's been a very long and strange day….

"I can arrange to be around for a very, very long time," he told her. Then he grinned. "I'd like to come in. But I understand perfectly. Okay, well, not perfectly, and I am disappointed, wishing I could be sleeping with you tonight."

She felt a flush touch her cheeks. "I didn't mean to…lead you on, to suggest…"

"You didn't. You're just the most fascinating woman I've met in aeons, and…hell, good night. I'll be around."

"I—well, I know you've been talking to David. We are divorced. There's just some ridiculous technicality."

"I'm not worried about a technicality," he told her.

"Neither am I."

"But I will step back if the technicality isn't just on paper, if it's something a lot deeper."

His words made her like him all the more. He wasn't about to step into the middle of a triangle, or be second-string to any other man.

"It's only a technicality—really." She meant to sound sincere. She wasn't sure if she really was or not. And she wasn't sure what he heard in her denial.

"Well..." he murmured.

He drew her to him, kissed her forehead. Then he walked down the steps, and started back along the foliage-bordered path.

She watched him disappear, realized she hadn't opened her door, and felt the pressure of the night and the shadows again. She quickly slid her key into the bolt for the glass doors, then stepped inside, feeling a rise of anger. She had never felt afraid here before, ever.

And now...

Though the image had faded for a moment due to skepticism and doubt, she could now vividly recall the corpse on the beach. A corpse that had disappeared.

She locked the door, making certain it was secure; then, still feeling an almost panicky unease, she walked through the little Florida room, kitchen and living room, assuring herself that windows were tightly closed and the front door was locked.

Damn David a million times over for both the trials haunting her tonight. If it hadn't been for him, John Seymore would be inside with her. Then she wouldn't be afraid of the shadows, or the memories stirring in her mind.

She slipped through the hallway to the first of the two

bedrooms in the cottage, the one she used for an office area. She checked the window there and even opened the closet door.

David's suggestion that she might be in danger seemed to be invading her every nerve. But the office was empty and secure.

Finally she went to her own room, found it safe, then prepared for bed and slipped under the covers. The night-light she kept on in the bathroom had always provided her with more than enough illumination, but tonight it only added to the shadows.

Usually the sound of the waves and the sea breeze rustling through the trees was soothing, but tonight…

She lay there for several seconds. Waves…breeze… palms. Foliage that seemed to whisper softly in the night, usually so pleasant…

A sudden thumping sound startled her so badly that she nearly screamed aloud. She did jump out of bed.

She'd heard a thump, as if something heavy had just landed on her roof.

She stood dead still, waiting. And waiting….

Nothing, no sound at all. Had she been deceived? The sound might have come from elsewhere….

Or might not have come at all.

She almost let out a loud sigh of pure frustration, but swallowed it back, and slowly, silently, tiptoed from her bedroom.

Into the hall…through to the kitchen. From there she could see both the living room and the little Florida room and the glass doors that led out back. The curtain was partially open. Had she left it that way?

The noise had come from the roof. There was a fireplace in the living area of each of the cottages. Despite the fact that this was sunny Florida, in the winter, during the few days that dipped into the forties or even the thirties, a fire was incredibly nice. But the chimney was far too small for a man to slip through.

So she was safe. There was nothing.

She was letting the simple sounds of nature slip into her psyche and scare her because she was still so unnerved by the happenings of the day.

A coconut had probably fallen off a palm. Still, just to be sure…

She walked to the back, trying to stay behind the curtain, then peeked out the glass. She pulled the drape back just a little more….

And screamed.

Chapter 4

Everyone was gone, Laurie thought. First Alex and John, then David. There were people around, but the Tiki Hut seemed empty. The band had reverted to calypso, very pleasant but also, in her current state of mind, sleep inducing.

Alex was crazy. She'd been married to David Denhem and divorced him.

Alex had never been to Date Tournament. Had she realized what was out there, she would undoubtedly still be married.

Maybe Alex thought that nights spent at a place like Date Tournament were simply not in her future. Then again, maybe she would never have such a night—because there was something about Alex that attracted men.

Laurie wished she had that innate…thing, whatever

it was. Maybe it would come with age, but Alex was only three years her senior. Well, maybe things weren't as perfect as they seemed for Alex, either.

"You're up late, aren't you?"

She started. It was Hank Adamson. She hadn't seen him before, but the Tiki Hut had been hopping, earlier, so he could have been lost in the crowd.

She saw Jay Galway on the other side of the bar, conversing with Seth Granger and a few of the other guests. He was staring at her—glaring, really—and giving her a big smile. Sign language, Jay Galway style. She was supposed to be as nice as possible, suck up big-time.

She gave an imperceptible nod to Jay and smiled as instructed at Hank. He slid out the chair opposite her and sat. "Okay if I join you and ask a few questions?"

"Sure."

In his lanky way, he was actually very attractive, she realized.

He grinned. "You look so wary."

"Do I? Well, we all know that the pen is very powerful."

"Update to computer," he said dryly.

"Okay, the written word—no matter how it's written."

"Honestly, you don't have to be so cautious. I didn't come to do a simple review. I'm going to do a whole piece on the place."

"A good piece—or a bad piece?"

"Good, bad…truthful."

"We're a good place," she said.

His grin deepened. "Actually, yes, Moon Bay does seem to follow through on every promise it makes. That's what's important. A little mom-and-pop establishment can get a great write-up, as long as it delivers on what it offers."

"Um, we're not exactly mom-and-pop," Laurie murmured.

"No, but so far, I've gotten a good bang for my buck, and that's what matters."

Laurie smiled. "That's great. I love Moon Bay. It's not just that I work here—I really love it. It's a wonderful place for a vacation."

"With the happiness and well-being of the guests foremost in everyone's mind at all times?"

"Yes, of course..." Laurie murmured, looking down at her hands suddenly. Was that true? What if that hadn't been a prank on the beach today? If Alex had been right, and a woman had been dead—and what if the killer had come back, aware that the body had washed up, and moved it?

"What is it?" She suddenly knew why Hank Adamson was considered so good. He asked casual questions; people gave casual answers. So casual you didn't realize that your mind was wandering off and that you were about to betray your real thoughts.

"What is what?" she asked innocently.

"You were about to say something. Do you feel that maybe, just sometimes, management isn't as concerned with safety as they should be? I'd never quote you by name."

Laurie stared at him and smiled slowly. "Well..." She leaned on the table, edging closer to him.

He did the same, anxious to hear whatever dirt she had to dish.

She leaned back. "Sorry, I don't have a bad thing to say about the place."

Adamson sat back, as well, obviously disappointed. He shook his head. "If there was something going on…something big, do you think that the employees would get wind of it?"

"Like what? The president arriving, or something like that?"

"No…like Moon Bay being involved in…something."

"Drugs? Here? Never," she assured him.

"I wasn't referring to drugs," he assured her.

She laughed softly. "Illegal immigrants? Not with Jay around. He wouldn't hire an illegal if his life depended on it."

"Not illegals," Hank said.

"Just what are you getting at?" she demanded.

"I don't know," he said. "I was hoping you did."

"That makes no sense. This is a resort, specially licensed for work with sea mammals. What could be going on?" Other than a body that appeared on the beach, then disappeared.

"Have you ever heard of a woman named Alicia Farr?" Adamson asked her.

"Sure. She's almost like a young, female Jacques Cousteau."

"Have you ever met her?"

"Nope. I think she's friends, kind of, with Alex. She's worked with David Denham. I'm pretty sure Jay Galway has worked with her, too."

"She hasn't been here, then, in the last couple of weeks?"

"Not unless she's been hiding in the bushes." Laurie was actually enjoying her conversation with him now. She'd had a few Tiki Hut specials, but she always watched her drinking here. And she could stand up to a grilling by a man like Hank Adamson. "Is she supposed to be here?"

"There was a rumor she was going to be, but I guess it wasn't true."

"I guess not."

"You're sure she's not here?" he persisted.

"There are private cottages here, twenty of them. Eight of them belong to the staff, and twelve are rented out. But this is an island. Room service is the only way to get food. There's a little convenience shop in the lobby, a boutique…but, honestly, I think it would be pretty hard for someone to hide out in one of the cottages. Maid service is in and out, engineering…. I'm pretty sure she wasn't here. We're off the Middle Keys, and there are lots of secluded places on the other islands. Maybe she's on one of them. I'm sorry to disappoint you—were you really trying to get a story on her?"

"I am doing an article on Moon Bay," he told her. "You know how it is, though. Lots of times, reporters get wind of a bigger story while they're in the middle of something more routine."

"So if you'd run into Alicia Farr here, that would have been nice, right?"

"It would have been interesting," he said. "You do know what she looks like, right? You'd know her if you saw her?"

"Sure. I've seen lots of articles on her. And I've seen her on television," Laurie said with a shrug.

She yawned suddenly, and quickly covered her mouth with her hand. "Sorry." She was. He was appealing in his lanky way, but he wasn't interested in her—

only what she might know. And she had no intention of telling him anything. She'd been ordered not to mention Alex's certainty that she'd seen a corpse, and she wouldn't.

She rose. "Please excuse me. Saturdays are very long here. People coming down from Dade County, locals who just like to come eat at the restaurant. The place is always busy."

He had risen along with her. "Thanks," he told her quietly.

"Sure. This place really is wonderful. I'm not lying, or just trying to keep my job by saying that. And Alex…well, there's no one better."

"So they say," he murmured, then asked politely. "Can I walk you to your cottage?"

"I don't rate a cottage—not yet," she told him with a shrug. "I just take the trail back to the fork in the road and head for the staff quarters. I'll be fine." She grinned to take the sting out of her next words, moved a step closer to him, and whispered, "Feel free to go question another employee. You'll find out every word I said was true."

He had the grace to flush. She gave him a wave and made her way past two couples on the dance floor, both a little inebriated, but heck, they weren't driving anywhere. If you were going to feel the influence of alcohol, this was the place to do it.

She could hear the band long after she had left the Tiki Hut behind. She started off thinking nothing of the night or the shadows, the trails were lit by torches—not like the ones at the Tiki Hut, which were real, but electrical torches made to give the grounds an island feel. Still…

Once the Tiki Hut was well behind her and the

noise from it had dimmed, she thought the night seemed especially dark. Strange, because her dad had shown her once before how the glow that radiated from Miami—sixty or seventy miles away, still extended this far when the sky was clear. But clouds were out tonight. It was storm season, of course. They'd had several nice days in the last week, though, she mused.

Nice days. A few with calm seas, a few others when the water was choppy. But then, the water didn't have to be wild to carry something—like a corpse—to the shore.

She stopped dead suddenly and instinctively, some inner defense aware of a rustling noise. She felt the hair rising at her nape.

She spun around. Nothing. But the bushes seemed to be very, very dark.

She had a sudden, vivid and ridiculous image of a corpse stalking her along the trail….

"Don't be ridiculous," she said aloud to herself.

But then…a rustling in the bushes…

She stared in the direction from which the noise had come, her heart racing a million miles an hour. Slowly, she made a circle where she stood, looking around.

The noise came again. She spun sharply, staring into the brush once again.

Then…a fat possum waddled out from the bushes and moved slowly across the path.

She let out her pent-up breath and giggled.

Then she turned, ready to set out along the path again. Instead she plowed into something dark and solid, and before her numbed mind could react, arms reached around her.

* * *

"Alex, for the love of God!"

David's voice was muted by the glass, but his impatience was evident. She was so relieved to realize that he was the figure on the porch that she didn't really think. She opened the sliding-glass doors, but she had to yell.

"You son of a bitch! What the hell are you doing out there? You nearly scared the life out of me."

He pushed his way in. It was dark, only the lights in front of the house illuminating the area around them. She could see that he still looked like a million bucks, dressed in dark chinos, a red tailored shirt and a light jacket.

She rued the fact that she was wearing a tattered T-shirt with the words "Moon Bay" embroidered in powder blue against a deep aqua background. She was equally sorry that it was very short. Silly. Even if they hadn't been married and she didn't have every inch of his anatomy etched into her memory forever, they spent their lives in bathing suits. She wondered why the T-shirt made her feel so naked. And vulnerable.

He walked through the cottage, checking the front door, looking around. "Is there any other way in here?" he asked, turning around slowly and studying the living room.

"Abracadabra?" she suggested.

"Cute, Alex. Is there any other way in here?"

"Front door, back door, as you can see."

He ignored her and headed for the small hallway that led to the bedrooms and bath.

"Hey!" she protested. She started to follow him, then paused, determined that the last place she wanted to be with him was a bedroom.

A moment later, he was back.

She frowned slightly, realizing he looked as if he had been running his fingers through his hair. She turned on the kitchen lights and stared at him once again. He looked tense. He reminded her of a shark, giving the impression of deceptive ease, while eyeing his prey to strike.

"What the hell are you doing?" she demanded.

"There was someone walking around your cottage, looking in the windows. I chased him around one side...and lost him," he told her.

"If there's anyone slinking around here," she said softly, "it's you."

He threw up his hands. "Alex, I'm serious."

"And I'm serious, too."

"Get this straight—I'm concerned."

Crossing her arms over her chest, she said firmly, "David, get this straight. You don't need to be concerned about me. I don't care about a technicality. We're not married anymore. I might not have been here alone."

"Actually, knowing you, you do care about a technicality," he informed her.

He was far too relaxed. "You followed me," she accused him. "You followed me when I was with another man, who was more than capable of taking care of me if I'd been in any danger."

"Alex, I don't really know that guy, and neither do you, and most important," he said very softly and seriously, "we are talking about a life-and-death situation."

She suddenly saw the man she knew from television, interviews and even, once upon a time, her personal life. The ultimate professional. Reeking of authority and command. Absolute in his conviction.

And for some reason, she shivered.

The woman on the beach had been dead. No matter what anyone tried to tell her. There had, beyond a doubt, been a corpse.

And it had disappeared.

"Maybe you'd like to explain it to me," she said.

He stared at her for a long moment. "I keep thinking you're better off, the less you know," he said quietly.

"Why? You already think I'm in some kind of danger."

"Yes, I do."

"Why?"

"You found a body on the beach. A body that disappeared."

She shook her head, watching him warily. "We've been through this. Jay and the sheriff were both certain I was duped."

"But you know it was true."

She wished so badly that she didn't feel such a desperate desire to keep her distance from him at all costs. Because she did know him. And she knew that he believed her. It wasn't necessary for him to have been there—he believed her.

"If you're so convinced, there must be a reason," she said flatly.

"Want to put some coffee on?" he suggested.

"No."

"Mind if I do?"

"Yes." Even as she spoke, she knew he would ignore her. He gave her a glance as if she was behaving like a spoiled child and moved into the kitchen. His arm brushed hers as he strode past her, and she felt as if she'd been burned.

Apparently he hadn't even noticed. He was heading for the cupboard above the coffeepot.

"Would you stop making yourself at home here, please?" she said, walking past him and shoving him out of the way. "I'll make coffee. You talk."

"What did she look like? The woman on the beach. What did she look like?"

She turned around and stared at him. "Like...a woman. Blonde."

"You didn't recognize her?" He stepped past her, impatiently taking the carafe and starting the coffee.

"Recognize her?" Alex said, startled.

"Yes, did you know who she might be?"

"No. She was at a strange angle. And she had long...or longish hair. It was covering her face. I touched her throat, looking for a pulse. And then...I don't know how to describe it exactly, but there was no way not to know she was dead."

"But you let them convince you that she couldn't have been, that you were wrong, and she just got up and walked away?" he demanded.

There was a note of disappointment in his tone.

"The sheriff was there," she told him sharply. "He doubted me. There was no body. What the hell was I supposed to do?"

He turned his back on her, opening a cupboard door.

"Cups are over here," she said impatiently, producing two from another cabinet.

He poured the coffee. He drank his black, so she was startled when he went to the refrigerator, absently taking out the milk to put a few drops into hers.

She accepted the coffee, watching him, feeling again

an embarrassed awareness of his crisp, tailored appearance and her own tattered T-shirt. Ridiculous to think about such things when they were talking about a corpse, she told herself.

"Did you mention your discovery to lover boy?" he inquired, sounding casual as he put the milk back in the refrigerator.

"I don't like your tone," she told him.

"Sorry, I don't like what's happening."

"Are you actually jealous?" she demanded.

"I'm not trying to run your life, if that's what you mean," he assured her. "I just don't like what's happening here."

"You haven't explained a damn thing yet, David."

"Did you tell him?" he persisted.

She let out a sigh of irritation. "No, but that doesn't mean I won't. For tonight…tonight I'm waiting. The sheriff will get back to us, let us know if anybody's missing from one of the ferries or the Middle Keys. He and Jay might have made me feel a little foolish today, but Nigel Thompson is a good man and no fool. And I could accuse you of many things, but being a total idiot isn't one of them. So get to it. What's going on?"

"I'm afraid I might know your corpse," he said quietly, his eyes a strange cobalt by night, and steady upon her.

Her heart seemed to skip a beat.

"Who?"

"Alicia Farr."

"Alicia?" she exclaimed. "Why…why would she be around here? There's not much to attract a woman of her reputation at a place like Moon Bay…but then again, there's not much here for you." She stopped speaking suddenly, staring at him. "I see. Great. You would have told me about this 'technicality' in the divorce, but only because it would have been convenient while you were here. You came to meet Alicia."

"No," he told her.

"You liar," she accused him softly. "Get out—now."

"I didn't come here just to meet her."

"David, I'll call security if you don't leave."

He arched an eyebrow, fully aware that "security" at Moon Bay meant two retired cops who were happy to putter around the grounds at night in retooled golf carts. There had never been serious trouble at Moon Bay—until today. And then they hadn't bothered with security; they had called the sheriff's department immediately.

"David, get the hell out."

"Alex, will you listen to me—I think Alicia is dead."

An eerie feeling crept along her spine. How could she be jealous of a corpse?

But she had been jealous of Alicia. The woman was—or had been—a free spirit, intelligent, beautiful and filled with knowledge, curiosity and a love of dangerous pursuits that nearly equaled David's own.

Could she be dead? That would be terrible.

But it wasn't sinking in. At the moment, Alex felt betrayed. She had to admit, it had felt nice to have David following her as if he was desperate.

"Alex?" he said, and his tone seemed to slip under her skin, no matter how numb she was suddenly feeling.

Then he walked over to her, put his cup down, and his hands went to her shoulders again, the whole of his length far too familiar against her own, his eyes piercing hers in a way she remembered too well. "Damn it, Alex, believe this—I don't want you ending up dead, as well."

They were talking about life and death, and all she felt was the texture of his jacket, the heat emanating from him. She breathed him in and remembered the way his hands could move. He was almost on top of her, and she felt a physical change in herself, a tautness in her breasts, with way too much of her body pressed there against his.

She wanted to shove him away—hard.

She managed to get a hand between them and place it firmly on his chest, pushing him away from her, and slipped from the place where she had been flush against the counter.

"Talk, David. Do it quickly. I have a nine o'clock dive in the morning, which means I have to be at the docks at eight."

Her voice sounded tight and distant. She wasn't sure if it was the effect she wanted or not. She should have been concerned, she knew, about Alicia. She had known the woman, after all, even admired her. But she hadn't liked her.

But that didn't mean she would have wanted harm to come to her. So why wasn't she more emotionally distressed? She was just too numb, unable to accept the possibility.

"Alicia called me a few weeks ago. Do you remember Danny Fuller?"

"Of course. He came here frequently, and he was charming." He had been. An octogenarian, the man had been in on the earliest days of scuba diving and helped in the later development of some of the best equipment available. He had loved dolphins, and that had naturally endeared him to Alex. "Yes, I knew Daniel fairly well. I was very sorry to hear he died about a month ago, at a hospital in Miami. Of natural causes."

"I know."

"They were natural causes, right?"

"Yes. But Alicia was with him a lot at the end."

"I can see it—him dying, and Alicia quizzing him about everything he knew until he breathed his last breath," Alex murmured. She hesitated. Alicia Farr was—or had been, if any of this was true—everything that she had not been herself. She found herself remembering the woman and the times they had worked together. Alicia was the epitome of a pure adventuress, courageous beyond sanity, at times. She was also beautiful.

Even before the last year, she had frequently appeared at David's side on TV and in magazines. He, naturally, thought the world of her.

He'd slept with her, certainly. But before or after the divorce? Alex had never been certain.

That must be why she was feeling so icy cold now. Good God, she didn't want the woman to be dead, but still…

"It's probably true that she pursued him mercilessly," David admitted. "But he also sent for her, so I guess she was the one he wanted to talk to in the end. At any rate, soon after he died, she called me. She said she was on to the biggest find of the century, and that she wanted me with her. And something she discovered had to do with Moon Bay." He seemed to notice the way Alex was staring at him. "Actually, I had already been toying with the idea of coming here, so it sounded fine to me. She set a date, and said that she would meet me here. Whether she made that same arrangement with anyone else or not, I don't know. But when I tried to get back to her, to confirm, I couldn't reach her. Then, when I got here, she was a no-show. I figured she'd gone ahead to check things out. You know Alicia when she's got the bit between her teeth. I still thought she'd show, though. But I did notice that the place seemed to be crawling with a strange assortment of visitors, including Seth Granger, Hank Adamson and your new friend—John Seymore. And then…I heard that you'd found a body on the beach."

For several long moments, Alex just stared at him, not at all sure what to think, or where to start. She felt chilled. She had found a body, and it could have been Alicia's.

No. Easier to believe Jay had been right. That she'd seen someone playing a sick—and very convincing—trick on someone else.

"Maybe Alicia just decided that she didn't want you in on her fabulous find after all. Maybe she's already off on her expedition," Alex said, her voice sounding thin.

"And maybe someone else found out what she had and killed her to get it—or before she could set up an expedition to recover the treasure, so they could get it for themselves."

"If there was really a body, it's gone now," Alex said. "And Sheriff Thompson—"

"I've spoken with him. He hasn't seen Alicia, and your corpse hasn't reappeared."

"Then…then you don't really have anything," Alex said.

"What I have is a tremendous amount of fear that a friend and colleague is dead—and that someone may now be after you. Alex, maybe there's someone out there who thinks you saw something, and that could put you in danger."

Alex shook her head. "David, I'm not going to start being paranoid because of the things that might be. If Alicia is dead, and someone was willing to kill her for what she knew, wouldn't you be in far more danger than I am? What about your own safety?"

"I can handle myself."

"Great. Handle yourself doing what? Waiting? Watching people?"

"I have friends looking for information now."

She stared at him. He had friends, all right. P.I.s, cops, law enforcement from around the world. And he was serious.

A slight shiver raked along her spine. If all this was true…

"All right, David. I appreciate your concern for my welfare. And I'm very sorry if Alicia is…dead. I know what she meant to you."

"No, actually, you don't."

He walked up to her, angry again, and she tensed against the emotion that seemed to fill him, though he didn't touch her.

"There was never anything intimate between Alicia and me. She was a good friend. That's all."

She didn't look up at him as she raised her hands. "Whatever your relationship…was, it's none of my business. As I said, thanks for your concern. I'll be very careful. I'll keep my eyes open, and I swear, if I hear anything, I'll tell you. Now, may I please go to sleep? Or try, at least, to get some sleep?"

"I can't leave you."

"What?"

"I can't leave you. Don't you understand? If someone out there thinks you can prove that Alicia is dead, that you might have seen…something, you're in danger of being murdered yourself."

She shook her head. "David, my doors lock. Please go away."

They were both startled when his phone suddenly started to ring. He pulled it from his pocket, snapping it open. "Denham," he said briefly.

She saw him frowning. "Sorry, say again. I'm not getting a great signal here."

He glanced at Alex in apology and walked out back, opening the sliding door, stepping out.

She followed after a moment. He was on the porch rocker, deep in conversation. She hesitated, then shut and locked the glass door. She was going to try to get some sleep. But how? Her mind was spinning.

Before she could reach the hallway, she heard a pounding on the glass. Then David's voice. "Damn it, Alex, let me in!"

"David, I'm fine. We'll talk tomorrow. Go away!"

"I won't leave you."

"Well, I won't let you in."

"I'll have to sleep on the porch then."

"Feel free."

She let the curtain fall closed. He slammed the glass with a fist. She was afraid for a minute it would shatter, despite the fact that it was supposedly hurricaneproof.

She stared at the drapes a long time. He didn't speak again, or hit the glass.

Maybe he had actually gone away. She forced herself to walk to her bedroom, lie down, close her eyes.

At some point, she finally slept.

Her alarm went off at six. She nearly threw it across the room. She felt as if she'd never actually slept, as if her mind had never had a chance to turn off.

After a second, she jumped out of bed and raced to the back, hesitated for a second, then carefully moved the curtain to look out.

David was just rising. To her absolute amazement, he had spent the night with his tall, muscular form pretzeled into the rattan sofa on the porch.

Suddenly she was afraid. Very afraid.

Chapter 5

David wasn't feeling in a particularly benign mood toward Alex, even after he had showered, gone back to his own cottage, downed nearly a pot of coffee, shaved and donned swim trunks, a T-shirt and deck shoes for the day. She'd really locked him out.

And gone to sleep without letting him back in.

He should have slept in his own bed. His cottage was next to hers—it just seemed farther because of the foliage that provided privacy and that real island feel that was such an advertised part of Moon Bay.

He hadn't gone to his own cottage, though, because he had seen someone snooping around her place. And the phone call he'd gone out to take hadn't been the least bit reassuring.

With that in mind, he pocketed his wallet and keys,

and left his cottage. Wanting to get out on the water ahead of the resort dive boat, he hurried down to the marina to board the *Icarus*.

As he started to loosen the yacht's ties, he heard his name being called.

Looking up, he saw John Seymore walking swiftly down the dock toward him. Hank Adamson and Jay Galway were following more slowly behind, engaged in conversation.

"Hey," he called back, sizing up Seymore again. For someone who had been spending his time diving the Pacific, he was awfully bronzed. That didn't mean anything in itself. The water on the West Coast might be cold as hell, but the sun could be just as bright as in the East.

"You're heading out early," John Seymore said. "Anywhere specific?"

"Just the usual dive sites," he replied. He realized that Seymore was angling for an invitation. Why not? "Are you booked on the resort's boat?"

"Couldn't get in—she was full," Seymore said cheerfully. "Hank had the same problem. We tried to weasel our way in through Jay, but he suggested we come down here to see what you had in store."

Just what he wanted. Jay Galway, Hank Adamson and Mr. Surf-Blond All-Around-Too-Decent-Guy out on the *Icarus* with him.

On the other hand, maybe not such a bad idea. He would know where the three of them were, and he might just find out what each of the men knew.

He shrugged. "Come aboard."

"I really appreciate the invitation," Seymore said. "Guys!" he shouted back loudly. "We're in!"

"Hop in, grab a line," David said.

John Seymore came on first, followed by Jay Galway, who hurried ahead of Hank Adamson. "Hey, thanks, David. Sincerely," Galway said. David nodded, figuring that Jay hadn't been happy about having to tell the writer that he couldn't get out for the day, even though it must look good for the resort's programs to be booked.

"This is damn decent of you," Adamson said, hopping on with agility. "Need some help with anything?"

"Looks like Jay has gotten the rest of the ropes. Make yourself at home."

"Want me to put some coffee on while we're moving out?" Jay asked.

"Good idea," David said.

"Sorry, I should have thought of that," John said, grimacing. "I always think of being on a yacht like this and drinking beer and lolling around on the deck."

"Oh, there's beer. Help yourself to anything in the galley." Just stay the hell out of my desk, he thought.

David kept his speed low as he maneuvered the shallow waters by the dock, then let her go. The wind whipped by as the *Icarus* cut cleanly through the water. Adamson and Seymore had remained topside with him, and both seemed to feel the natural thrill of racing across the incredible blue waters with a rush. When they neared the first dive spot on the reef, he slowed the engine.

"Trust me to take the helm?" Seymore asked him.

"Sure," David said, giving him the heading briefly, then hopping down the few steps that led to the cabin below.

He glanced around quickly, assuring himself that his computer remained untouched and it didn't appear Galway had been anywhere near his desk, which was in the rear of the main cabin in a mahogany enclave just behind the expansive dining table and the opposing stretch of well-padded couch.

"Good timing. Coffee's ready," Jay told him. Jay knew the *Icarus*. He'd once gone out with David on a salvage expedition, when he'd been going down to the wreck of a yacht lost in storm, the *Monday Morning*. The boat had been dashed to pieces, but she'd carried a strongbox of documents her corporate owners had been anxious to find. It had been a simple recovery, but Galway had been elated to be part of the process.

"Thanks," David said.

Jay handed him a cup of black coffee. "For a good-looking son of a bitch, you look like hell this morning," Jay told him.

"I didn't sleep well."

Jay poured himself a cup. "Me neither."

"Dreaming about corpses?"

Jay didn't look startled by the question. "There was no corpse," he said flatly.

"Not when you got there," David suggested.

Jay shook his head. "I asked Alex not to say anything—since we didn't have a body."

"She didn't."

"Then?"

"It's an island, a very small one," David reminded him.

"I was sure Laurie would have the good sense to keep quiet when I asked her to," Jay said disgustedly.

"Laurie didn't talk. Things…get around."

"So you're not going to tell me where you got your information?" Jay asked.

"Nope."

"Like I said, there was no body," Jay told him. He frowned. "How far do you think it's gotten around?"

"Who knows?"

Jay groaned. "If the guests start to hear this…"

"I don't think it'll get around to the rest of the guests," David assured him. God, the coffee was good.

"It was Len, wasn't it? And don't deny it."

"Doesn't matter how I know. And I haven't said a word to anyone else. I know Alex hasn't either, and I'd almost guarantee Laurie hasn't. I do have a question for you. What makes you so convinced Alex was duped?"

Jay looked at him. His surprise seemed real. "There was no body there. And corpses don't get up and walk."

"They can be moved."

"I'm not an idiot. I was looking around just like the sheriff. The sheriff. We didn't just call security and forget it. We called the sheriff. There was no sign of a body ever having been there or being taken away. There were no footprints and no drag marks."

"What the hell does that mean? Someone strong enough could throw a woman's body over his shoulder—and there are palms fronds around by the zillions. Footprints on a beach could easily be erased."

"There couldn't have been a body," Jay said.

David watched him for a few minutes. Jay wasn't meeting his eyes. Instead he seemed intent on wiping the counter where nothing had spilled.

"You look like you're afraid there might have been. And worse, you look as if you're afraid you know who it could have been," David said softly.

Jay stared at him then. “Don’t be insane! I’d never kill anyone.”

“I didn’t say you would. You know, I asked you before about Alicia Farr. You assured me that she hadn’t checked in to the resort.”

“She hasn’t,” Jay protested.

“She was supposed to be here.”

“She called about a possible reservation, but she never actually booked. I didn’t think she would. It’s not her cup of tea. Anyway, that was it. She called once, made sure I had the dates available that she wanted, then said she’d get back to me. She didn’t. That’s the God’s honest truth. She never called back.”

It sounded as if Jay was sincere, but David couldn’t be certain.

Jay gasped suddenly, staring at David. “I know what you’re thinking! Believe me, there couldn’t have been a corpse. And if there was…it couldn’t have been Alicia. I mean, she didn’t check in. She was never on the island.”

“Well, if there wasn’t a corpse, it couldn’t have been anyone, right? But I should tell you, Alicia was in Miami a week ago, where she rented a boat and said she was heading down to one of the small private islands in the Keys.”

“Do you know how many small private islands there are down here? Maybe she intended to come here but changed her mind. She must have arranged to go somewhere else—maybe a place that belongs to a friend or something.” His eyes narrowed. “Were you…with her? In Miami?”

David shook his head.

“How do you know what she was doing, then?”

"She called me. Then when I called back and couldn't reach her I had a friend do a trace on her."

"Alicia is independent. She knows her way around."

"When she called me, she asked me to meet her here, at Moon Bay. The way she talked, she was excited about seeing Moon Bay. She seemed very specific. When she called you, she didn't say anything about her reason for coming?"

"I swear, she didn't tell me anything. She was pleasant and asked about available dates, and that was all," Jay assured him, then frowned. They could both see Hank Adamson's deck shoes, then his legs, as he descended into the cabin.

"Mind if I take a look around her?" he asked David.

"Hell no. I'm proud of my girl and delighted to give you a tour. Jay, how about relieving John at the helm, so he can get a good look at the *Icarus*, too?"

"Sure. I already know my way around," Jay told Adamson. There was a note of pride in his voice. David watched him thoughtfully as he headed topside.

Jay Galway had been sweating when they talked. A little sheen of perspiration had shown on his upper lip.

So…

Either he was afraid, or he was lying.

Or both.

Alex had expected Zach to be a problem.

He wasn't. The teenager duly handed her his dive card, then sat through her reminders and instructions like an angel. His mom had decided to stay on shore, despite the fact that they were going to make a stop on one of the main islands before returning that night.

Doug Herrera was captaining their dive boat, and Mandy Garcia was Alex's assistant. They all switched between dive excursions and the dolphins. Gil and Jeb were dealing with the morning's swim, and Laurie was taking her day off. Actually, Alex had expected to see her friend at the docks anyway—Laurie loved to dive, and she especially loved a day when the boat was scheduled to make a stop on one of the main islands when she wasn't working. It was a chance to check out the little waterside bar where they had a meal and after-dive drinks, for those who chose, before returning to Moon Bay.

But Laurie had still been at the Tiki Hut when Alex left, so maybe the late night and the excitement of the day had caused her to sleep in. And maybe she had decided not to come because Seth Granger was on the dive, and he always made things miserable.

At Molasses Reef, their first dive, Alex noted that the *Icarus*, David's yacht, was already anchored nearby. They never anchored on the reefs themselves. Most divers were aware of the very delicate structure of the reef and that it shouldn't be touched by human hands, much less bear the weight of an anchor, and wouldn't have moored there even if there hadn't been laws against it. David was close though, closer than they went themselves.

"Now that's a great-looking yacht," Seth commented, spitting on his mask to prep it.

"Yes," she agreed. The *Icarus* was a thirty-two footer, and she looked incredible under full sail. Today, however, David wasn't sailing her. He'd apparently used the motor. The yacht moved like a dream, either way. Inside, the mahogany paneling and rich appointments made her just as spectacular. The galley had every possible accessory, as did the captain's desk. She was big enough to offer private sleeping facilities for up to three couples.

"You should have asked for the yacht," Seth said, eyeing the *Icarus*.

"I beg your pardon?"

"In your divorce settlement. You should have asked for the yacht. She's a beauty. But, hey, you've got another chance to ask for her now. Heard you're not really divorced," Seth said.

"Where did you hear that?"

He laughed again, or rather, bellowed. "People talk, you know. Moon Bay is an island. Small. People talk. About everything."

He stared at her, which gave her a very uncomfortable feeling. What else was being discussed?

"I don't want her. She belongs to David. Now, if you'll excuse me, I have to get in the water. And so do you. The tour group is waiting."

Her people were buddied up the way she'd arranged them after she'd duly studied their certificates and discussed their capabilities. She'd decided to buddy up with Zach herself.

In the water, leading the way, even though she was checking constantly to assure herself that her group indeed knew what they were doing and how to deal with their equipment, she found a certain peace. The sound of her own air bubbles always seemed lulling and pleasant. As yet, no cell phones rang here.

Zach stuck with her, amazed. A Michigan kid, he'd gotten his certificate in cold waters and was entranced by the reef. It was a joy to see his pleasure in the riot of tropical fish, and in the giant grouper that nosily edged their way.

This was an easy dive; most of it no more than thirty feet. When she counted her charges again, she saw that Seth Granger had wandered off. His "buddy," the mother of the girls from the day before, was looking lost.

Alex motioned to Zach, then went after Granger. He seemed hostile, but, to her relief, he rejoined the group.

Back on deck, he was annoyed. "I saw David out on the reef. I was just going over for a friendly underwater hello."

"Mr. Granger—"

"Seth. Come on, honey, we've seen enough of each other."

"Seth, if you'd wanted an unplanned, individual dive, you should have spoken with David earlier—and gone out on the *Icarus* with him. I'm sure he'd have been happy to have you."

"Don't be ridiculous. You know I know what I'm doing in the water."

"Guess what, Seth? I don't go diving alone. Too dangerous. Now, I can have the skipper take the boat back in and drop you off at Moon Bay, or you can stay with the group and abide by our rules."

He pointed a finger at her. "I'll be talking to your boss tonight."

"You do that."

At the next two stops, he still wandered, but not as badly, as the first time pretending he had become fascinated by a school of tangs and followed them too far, and then, on the last go-round, that he had seen a fantastic turtle and been unable to resist.

When the last dive was completed, Alex allowed herself a moment's pleasure. Zach was in seventh heaven, and her other divers were exuberant over the beauty they had witnessed. They were ready, when they reached the main island and the little thatch-roofed diner, to eat, drink and chat.

"Good job, boss lady!" Jeb commented to her, a sparkle in his eye, as they went ashore themselves. "How about you have a nice dinner, and I'll keep Seth out of your hair?"

Jeb was great. A college senior, he was only hers for the summer. He was a thin kid, with flyaway dark hair, and a force and energy that defied his bony appearance. He never argued with her, watched her intently all the time, and was one of those people who seemed intent on really learning and absorbing all the information they could. When she wasn't working with Laurie, she was happiest with Jeb, though all her assistants were handpicked and great.

"You're on," she told him gratefully.

Leaving the dive boat to her captain, Alex made certain all her charges were comfortable at the Egret Eatery, as the little restaurant was called.

Zach had already found the video games located at the rear of the place. The adults had settled in at various tables.

She saw Jay, Hank, John and David at a table and felt a moment's wary unease. The four of them had obviously spent the day out on the reef together. She'd known the *Icarus* was a stop ahead of her all day. She just hadn't realized how full the yacht had been.

She was about to venture toward their table, but

then she saw Seth Granger moving that way, so she steered clear.

"Hey, guys," Seth bellowed. "Mind if I join you? Drinks on me. What'll it be?"

"A pitcher of beer would be appreciated," Hank told him.

"Coke for me," David said.

"Come on. You're not going to crash after one beer, buddy."

"No, a Coke will do fine for me." David looked up and caught Alex's eyes across the room. She felt a chill leap across the open space. For a man so determined to see to her safety, he looked a lot like he wanted to throttle her. Apparently he hadn't enjoyed his night on the porch.

But he had stayed there. And he believed her, believed that the body she had discovered was Alicia Farr's, and that she herself might well be in real danger.

But from who?

Since she wasn't captaining any boat, she turned to the bar and asked Warren, the grizzled old sailor who owned the place, for a beer.

"Sure thing, Alex. How's it going over there? It's been a little slow around here."

"Really? I'm not sure about the hotel, but the dives and swims have been full," she told him.

Setting her glass down, he pointed at the television. "Storm season."

"Summer is always slower than winter. Northerners stay home and sweat in their own states during the summer," she reminded him.

He grinned. "Maybe, but we usually get a bigger Florida crowd around here than we've been getting lately."

She glanced at the TV above the bar. “Is something going on now? I haven’t seen any alerts. The last tropical storm out veered north, right?”

“Yep. Now there’s a new babe on the horizon. She just reached tropical-storm status, and she’s been named Dahlia, but they think she’s heading north, too. They think she might reach hurricane status sometime, but that she’ll be off the Carolinas by then. Still, people don’t seem to be venturing out as much as usual. Thank God you bring your guests over here. Right now, frankly, you’re helping me survive.”

“Don’t worry. I’m sure business will pick up,” she assured him.

“I see your ex is here. It’s always good for business when he shows up here. Word gets out, makes people feel like they’re coming to a real ‘in’ place. Still, it’s kind of a surprise to see him. You all right?”

“Of course. We’re still friends on a professional level,” Alex said.

“You know what I think?” Warren asked her.

“What?”

He leaned low against the bar. “I think he came here for you.”

“Mmm,” she said. Me, and whatever excitement and treasure Alicia had in store, she thought, but she remained silent on the subject.

Then she asked, “Warren, you know who Alicia Farr is, right? Has she been around?”

“Nope, not that I’ve heard about.”

“Well, thanks.”

“Who’s the blond Atlas with your ex?” Warren asked.

“Tourist.”

"Not your typical tourist," Warren commented, wiping a bar glass dry.

"No, I agree." She shrugged. "Thanks, Warren," she told him. The place was thatch-roofed and open, but she suddenly needed more air. She took her beer and headed outside. She walked along the attached dock, where the dive boat had pulled in, came to the end and looked out at the water, studying the *Icarus*.

She wasn't docked; David had anchored her and come in by way of the dinghy. A moment's nostalgia struck her. She had really loved the *Icarus*, and she did feel a pang that the beautiful sailing vessel wasn't a part of her existence anymore.

She had fair compensation in her life, she knew. Diving, here off the Florida coast, would always be a joy, no matter who was on the tour. And she had her dolphins. They might actually belong to the corporation that owned Moon Bay, but they were her babies. Shania, especially. Wounded, just treated and beginning to heal when Alex had come on board, the adolescent dolphin was her favorite—though, naturally, she'd never let the other dolphins know. But she felt as if she and Shania had gained trust and strength at the same time. She had noticed that Shania followed her sometimes. One night, sipping a drink at the Tiki Hut, she had looked up to find the dolphin, nose above the surface, watching her from the lagoon.

And she had learned to live alone. By the end of her whirlwind one-year marriage to David, she had been alone most of the time anyway. Her choice, she reminded herself in fairness. But he never wanted to stay in one place, and she had longed to establish a real base, a real home. Too many times, he had been with a woman who shared his need for constant adventure. Like Alicia Farr. And she had let the doubts slip in and take over. When she had filed the papers and he hadn't said a single word, she had forced herself to accept the truth—she wasn't what he wanted or needed. He had Alicia, and others like her.

He had been planning on meeting Alicia at Moon Bay. And now he suspected she was dead.

With that thought, she dug into the canvas bag she'd brought ashore, found her cell and called the sheriff's office. She was certain she was going to have to leave a message, but Nigel Thompson's assistant put her right through.

"Hey, Alex."

"Hey, Nigel. I'm sorry to bother you, but…I'm concerned."

"Of course. But listen, I checked all the ferry records. No one's missing. Everyone who checked into Moon Bay is alive and well and accounted for. And all the day-trippers and people who checked out of Moon Bay were on the ferries out. Usually there are people in their own boats who come by way of the Moon Bay marina, but not yesterday."

"Thanks, Nigel," she murmured.

"Alex?"

"Yeah."

"I don't think you're easily fooled. I sent some men out last evening to walk the grounds. But they didn't find anything."

"Thank you, Nigel. I guess…I don't know. Thank you anyway."

"Sure thing."

She snapped the phone closed.

She nearly jumped a mile when a hand fell on her shoulder. She spun around, spilling half her beer.

It was just Jeb.

"Sorry," he said quickly. "I didn't mean to startle you. I saw you go out, so I followed. Want to wander into a few shops with me? I need a tie."

"You need a tie?"

He grimaced. "A friend is getting married up in Palm Beach next week. I've got the makings of a suit, but I don't own a single tie."

Her own thoughts were driving her crazy, but she couldn't think of a rational step she could take to solve any of her dilemmas. Might as well go tie shopping.

"So…where's that new girl of yours, David?" Seth asked.

They hadn't been there long; but Seth Granger had already consumed five or six drinks—island concoctions made with three shots each.

David had never particularly liked the guy to begin with, and with a few drinks in him, he was pretty much completely obnoxious.

"New girl?" David asked.

"Alicia Farr. Fair Alicia. Since the wife threw you over after all those pictures of the two of you came out, I figured the two of you were an item. She isn't here with you, huh? I heard tell she had something up her sleeve and was going to be around these parts. Word is she learned something from that old geezer who died a while back. Danny Fuller."

David wondered if Seth Granger was really drunk or was just pretending to be. He'd spent the day listening, waiting for one of his guests to ask the right question, make the right slip. No go. They might have been any four good old boys out for a day on the water.

But now…

"Sorry, Seth. Alicia and I were never an item. We team up now and then for work. We have a lot of the same interests, that's all. There's no reason for her to be at Moon Bay."

"Actually, there was an article about her in the news a few weeks back. Of course, it was in one those supermarket tabloids, so… Anyway, the headline was something like Dying Mogul Gives Secrets to Beauty Who's a Beast. The writer seemed to think she'd been hanging on him hoping to get news on any unclaimed treasure he might know about. There was a definite suggestion that she was coming to the Keys."

Jay Galway thumped his beer stein on the table a little too hard. "So why do you think she was headed for Moon Bay? There are two dozen islands in the Keys."

"That's true enough," David said, eyeing John Seymore. "So you're up on the movements of Alicia Farr, too, huh?" he inquired, forcing a bit of humor into his voice.

"I'm a wannabe, I admit," John said ruefully.

"I know what it takes to be a SEAL," David commented. "I can't imagine you're a wannabe anything."

"Not like me, huh?" Seth Granger demanded, giving David a slap on the back that caught him totally unaware and awakened every fighting reaction inside him.

He checked his temper. "Hell, Granger, with your money? I doubt you're a wannabe anything, either."

"The wannabe would be me," Jay said dryly.

"Jay, you're running a four-star resort, and your vacations are pure adventure," David assured him.

"Yeah, but I bust my butt for all of them—and I'm still on the fringes. But you know…I spent a lot of time with Danny Fuller. I'm sure he had a dozen treasure maps stored in his head, things he learned over the years, and Alicia had the looks—and the balls. So…"

"Looks like we're all here looking for Alicia," Seth said. "And she's blown us all off."

"I don't actually know her," John Seymore reminded them.

"That's right—Seymore's just here to get warm and cuddly with the sea life," David said.

"And your ex-wife," Seth commented.

A tense silence suddenly gripped the table.

Then David's phone rang, as if on cue. "Excuse me, will you?" he said to the others. "Reception is better outside."

He rose, flipping open the phone as he walked out, then paused in the alleyway outside the little restaurant, shaded by a huge sea grape tree.

"Can you talk?" his caller asked.

"You bet," David said. "I've been hoping to hear from you."

"I spent some time at the hospital where Danny Fuller died. Seems Alicia was in on an almost daily basis. One of the nurses heard her swearing to Danny again and again that she wasn't after money, just discovery. And whatever Danny told her, it had to do with dolphins. Apparently the words dolphin and lagoon came up over and over again. And there was one more thing I think you'll find of interest." The man on the other end paused.

"What's that?" David asked after a long silence. Dane Whitelaw didn't usually hesitate. An ex–special-forces agent, he had opened his own place in Key Largo, where he combined dive charters with a private investigation firm. Sounded a bit strange, but it seemed to work out well enough. He avoided a lot of the big city slush and came up with some truly interesting work, a lot of it to do with boats lost at sea and people who disappeared after heading out for the Caribbean.

Some of them wanted to disappear.

Some of them were forced to do so.

But if he needed information of any kind, David had never met anyone as capable as Dane of finding it out.

Dane was still silent.

"You still there?" David asked.

"Yeah."

"Well?"

"Apparently, according to the old guy's night nurse, your ex-wife's name kept coming up, as well."

"What?"

"She said the two kept talking about an Alex McCord."

David digested the information slowly. Finally it was Dane's turn to ask, "Hey, David, you still there?"

"Yeah, yeah. I need another favor."

"What's that?"

"Look into a guy for me. If he's telling the truth at all, you should be able to dig up some stuff on him."

"Sure. Who's the guy?"

"An ex–navy SEAL. John Seymore."

* * *

Jeb had his tie. Alex wasn't certain what it was going to look like when combined with a dress shirt and a jacket, but it was certainly a comment about the lifestyle he loved. Light blue dolphins leaping against a cobalt background.

Alex had purchased one of the same ties. Reflex action, she decided. The darker color was just like David's eyes, and she used to buy all kinds of little things just because they might appeal to him.

"Damn," she murmured as they walked back to the restaurant.

"What?"

"Oh…nothing. I guess I don't really want to go back in and see our…group." Nor did she want to pass the alley. She could see David. He was bare chested, wearing deep green trunks and deck shoes, leaning against the wall. He hadn't noticed them yet, because he was too deeply engrossed in a telephone conversation.

"Our group? Oh, you mean Seth Granger," Jeb suggested.

She shrugged. "Right. Seth." Seth was just a pain in the butt, though. Annoying to deal with, but once she was away from him, she forgot all about him.

She really didn't want to see David. She was furious with herself for having instinctively bought the tie.

"Just walk on by then, Alex. The boat is at the end of the dock. Wait there. I'll go in and gather up the forces. Hopefully anyone who wandered off shopping is back. And hopefully those who did more drinking than eating won't be too inebriated."

She smiled and thanked him, then started down the

dock. The sunset was coming in, and she believed with her whole heart that nothing could compare to sunset in the Florida Keys. The colors were magnificent. If there was rain on the horizon, they were darker. On a bright day like today, the night came with a riot of unparalleled pastels.

It was her favorite time of day. Peaceful. Especially when she had a few moments alone, as she did now. The dock was empty. The other boaters docked nearby were either on shore or in their cabins. The evening was hers.

She strolled the length of rustic wood planks and, at the end, stretched and sat, dangling her feet as she appreciated the sky and tried not to think about the corpse she had seen.

Or the husband she had so suddenly reacquired.

"Who's missing here?"

David had just reentered the restaurant in time to hear Jeb Larson's question.

"Mr. Granger," Zach called out helpfully.

"Mr. Denham," Jeb asked, spotting David. "Have you seen Mr. Granger?"

"Sorry, I went out to make a call. He was at the table when I left."

Jay Galway came striding in at that moment, a bag bearing the name of a local shop in his hand. He arched an eyebrow at Jeb. "Got a problem?"

"Just missing a diver," Jeb said, never losing his easy tone. "Mr. Granger."

Jay seemed startled as he looked around. "He was here twenty minutes ago," he said. "David?"

"Don't know. I was on the phone."

"He said something about going out for a smoke," Hank Adamson called. He was standing at the end of the bar. David was certain he hadn't been there a minute ago.

He looked around. John Seymore seemed to be among the missing, as well, but just then he came striding in from around back.

"Excuse me, Mr. Seymore," Jeb called. "Have you seen Mr. Granger?"

"Nope," John Seymore said.

"Leave it to Granger."

The words were a bare whisper of aggravation, but David was close enough to Jay Galway to hear them.

"Well, relax...we'll find him," Jeb said, still cheerful.

"Maybe he went shopping," Zach suggested.

"Yep, maybe," Jeb said, and tousled the boy's hair.

"You know," David said quietly to Jay, "they can take the dive boat on back. We can wait for him."

Jay cast him a glance that spoke volumes about his dislike for the man, but all he said was, "We can wait a few minutes."

Alex stared at the lights as they played over the water. The lapping sound of the sea as it gently butted against dozens of hulls and the wood of the dock pilings was lulling. The little ripples below her were growing darker, but still, there was a rainbow of hues, purple, deepest aqua, a blue so dark it was almost ebony.

She frowned, watching as something drifted out from beneath the end of the dock where she sat.

At first, she was merely puzzled. What on earth...?

Then her blood ran cold. She leaped to her feet, staring down. Her jaw dropped, and she clenched her throat to scream…caught the sound, started to turn, stopped again.

No. This body wasn't disappearing.

And so she went with her first instinct and began to scream as loudly as she could.

"We all have to wait here for just one guy?" one of the divers complained.

"My Mom will be getting worried," Zach said.

"Don't worry, you can use my phone," David assured the teen, handing it to him. "Don't you have a cell phone?" he asked the boy.

Zach grinned. "You bet. But Mom wouldn't let me take it on the boat. Said I might lose it overboard. She doesn't dive," he said, as if that explained everything about his mother.

"Leave it to Seth Granger," Jay said, and this time, he was clearly audible. "Go ahead," he instructed Jeb. "You and the captain and Alex get our crew back. David has said he doesn't mind waiting for Granger." He turned to David. "You're sure?" he asked.

"Sure. We'll wait," he said, and he hoped to hell it wasn't going to be long. Now, more than ever, he didn't want Alex out of his sight.

The others rose, stretched and started to file out.

And that was when they heard the scream.

Somehow, the instant he heard it, David knew they weren't going to have to wait for Granger after all.

Chapter 6

Everyone came running.

Alex wasn't thrilled about that, but after her last experience, she'd had to sound an alarm—she wasn't letting this body drift away. Before the others came pounding down the dock, though, she dived in. Though the man was floating face downward and sure as hell looked dead, she wasn't taking any chances.

The water right by the dock was far from the pristine blue expanse featured in tourist ads. She rose from a misty darkness to grab hold of the man's floating arm.

With a jolt, she realized it was Seth Granger.

By then the others had arrived. David was in the lead and instantly jumped into the water to join her. He was stronger and was easily able to maneuver the body. John Seymore, with Jeb at his side, reached down as David pushed Seth upward; between them, they quickly got Seth Granger lying on the dock, and, despite the obvious futility, Jeb dutifully attempted resuscitation. Alex heard someone on a cell phone, telling a 911 operator what had happened. By the time she and David had both been fished out of the water and were standing on the dock, sirens were blaring.

Jeb, youthful and determined, kept at his task, helped by John, but Seth was clearly beyond help.

He still reeked of alcohol.

Two med techs came racing down the dock, and when they reached Seth Granger, Jeb and John stepped aside. The men from Fire Rescue looked at one another briefly, then took over where John and Jeb had left off.

"Anyone know how long he's been in the water?" one of them.

"Couldn't be more than twenty minutes," John Seymore said. "He was definitely inside twenty minutes ago."

"Let's get him in the ambulance, set up a line…give him a few jolts," one of the med techs said. In seconds, another team was down the dock with a stretcher, and the body was taken to the waiting ambulance.

Then the sheriff arrived. He didn't stop the ambulance, but he looked at Seth Granger as he was taken away, and Alex noted the imperceptible shake of his head. He took a deep breath and turned to the assembled crowd.

"What happened?" Nigel Thompson demanded.

"Well, he was drinking too hard and too fast, that's for sure," Hank Adamson commented.

"We were at a table together," Jay told Nigel. He pointed around. "Seth, John, Hank, David and myself.

David's phone rang, and he decided to take it outside. I needed to pick up a few things, so I headed down the street, and then..." He looked at the other two who had shared the table.

"I went to the men's room," John Seymore said, and looked at Hank Adamson.

"I walked up to the bar."

"When did Granger leave the bar?" Nigel asked.

His answer was a mass shrugging of shoulders.

"Hell," Nigel muttered. "All right, everyone back inside."

David was already on his feet. He reached a hand down to Alex, his eyes dark and enigmatic. She hesitated, then accepted his help.

She realized, as she stood, that John Seymore was watching. He gave her a little smile, then turned away. It seemed that day suddenly turned to night. She shivered, then regretted it. David slipped an arm around her shoulders. "You all right?" he asked.

"Of course," she said coldly.

"Alex, you don't have to snap," he said softly.

She removed his arm from around her shoulders and followed the others. She meant to find wherever John was sitting and take a place beside him.

Too late. Zach was on John's left, Hank Adamson on his right. There was one bench left, and there was little for her to do other than join David when he sat there.

She suddenly felt very cold, and, gritting her teeth, she accepted the light windbreaker he offered. She instantly regretted the decision. It felt almost as if she had cloaked herself in his aura. It wasn't unpleasant. It was too comfortable.

The sheriff's phone rang. "Thompson," he said briefly as he answered it. A second later, he flipped his phone closed. "Well, it's bad news but not unexpected. He was pronounced dead at the hospital."

"Mind if we go over Mr. Granger's movements one more time?" Nigel asked.

"He came, he drank, he fell in the water," a businessman who'd been on the dive said impatiently.

"Thanks for the compassion, sir," Nigel said.

"Sorry, Sheriff," the man said. "But the guy was rich and being a rude pain in the you-know-what all day."

"Well, thank goodness not everyone who's rude ends up drowning," the sheriff said pointedly. "I'd have myself one hell of a job," Nigel commented.

"Sorry," the man said again. "It's just that…we're all tired. I only met the man today on the dive, and he wasn't the kind of person to make you care about him. And I'm on vacation."

"Well, then, I'll get through this just as fast as I can. First things first—those of you from Moon Bay. Anyone checking out tomorrow?"

No one was, apparently. Or, if so, they weren't about to volunteer the information.

"Good. Okay, I'm going outside. One by one, come out, give me your names, room numbers and cell-phone numbers, and I may have a quick question or two. Then you can reboard and get going."

Squeaky wheels were the ones oiled first, Alex determined. Nigel asked her whining diver to come out first.

"This is kind of silly," a woman who had been on the dive complained. "A pushy rich man got snockered and fell in the water. That's obvious."

"Nothing is obvious," David said, his eyes focused on the woman. Alex felt the coiling heat and tension in his body before he continued. "Nigel Thompson is top rate. He's not leaving anything to chance."

The woman flushed and fell silent.

Alex felt as if she were trapped, so aware of David in the physical sense that she was about to scream. In this room full of people, in the midst of this tense situation, she found herself focusing on the most absurd things. Like her ex-husband's toes. His muscled calves. Legs that were long and powerful. When he inhaled, his flesh brushed hers.

She forced herself to look across the room at John Seymore, instead.

In the room, conversations began. David turned to Alex suddenly. "You all right?" he asked softly.

"Of course I'm all right," she said. He was studying her gravely. Then a slight smile curved his lips. "Why?" she asked cautiously.

His head moved closer. His lips were nearly against her ear. When he spoke, it seemed that his voice and the moisture of his breath touched her almost like a caress. "You've been undressing me with your eyes," he told her.

"You are undressed," she informed him. "And what I'm thinking about is the fact that a man drowned."

"Did he?"

"Of course! Damn you, David, we were both there."

"We were both there to pull the body out of the water, but we weren't there when he died."

"He drowned," she insisted.

"Isn't this getting to you just a little bit?" His voice lowered even further. "You're in danger."

"And you're going to protect me?" she demanded.

"You bet."

"Are you going to keep sleeping on my porch?"

"No, you're going to let me into the cottage."

"Dream on. I don't know what this absurd obsession with me is, but do you really think you're going to scare me into letting you back in my bed?"

"Only if you insist, and if it will make you feel better."

In that moment she hated him with a sudden intensity, because she had been so secure, so ready to explore a relationship with another man, and now…

David had played on her mental processes. She knew he could make her feel secure…that his flesh against her own could feel irresistibly erotic, compelling…. She wanted to curl against him, close her eyes, rest, imagine.

"You've got some explaining to do, too," he informed her. Suddenly his eyes reminded her of a predatory cat.

She stiffened. "I have to explain something to you?"

"About Danny Fuller."

"Danny Fuller?"

They both fell silent.

As more people filed outside, those waiting to be questioned began to shift around. Alex saw her opportunity and rose, placing as much distance as she could between herself and David.

And then, with nothing else to do, she found herself pacing the room. Danny Fuller? What the hell was he talking about?

She was idly walking in front of one of the long benches when she nearly collided with Jay. He caught hold of her shoulders to steady her, then sighed, turned and took a seat on the bench right behind him.

She gazed at him where he sat. His hands were steepled prayer fashion in front of him, and he was looking upward. "Thank you, God," he barely whispered. "Thank you for making this happen here and not on Moon Bay."

"Jay!" she gasped, horrified.

He looked up at her and flushed. "Well, he was a mean old bastard, and he'd lived out most of his life," Jay protested. "He liked to drink way too hard, and never believed the sea could be stronger than he was. Well, you can't turn up your nose and think you're better than the Atlantic."

"This is still horrible."

"Yeah, I'm sure all his ex-wives are going to be crying real hard," Jay murmured.

She started to say something, then fell quiet. Without her noticing, the room had been emptying out.

It was just her and Jay left to speak with the sheriff, and Nigel was coming toward them.

"Well, it's a miracle, but no one in this place saw Seth Granger walk out. No one. Not the bartender, not a single waiter, waitress, busboy, cook or floor scrubber, none of the locals, and certainly none of your guests from Moon Bay."

"Nigel, the guy was drunk," Jay said wearily.

Nigel shook his head. "Seth Granger was always drinking, from what I've heard. Strange that he would just walk into the water, though. Stranger still that no one saw him do it. Never mind." He pointed a finger at Alex. "I want to talk to you at some length. Tomorrow. Got it?"

"Me?"

"Two days, two bodies," Nigel said.

"But…you told me there was no second body. Or first body. Other body."

"Alex, I already told you, I did all the checking I could—and I sent men out to walk the grounds. You know I didn't discount your story entirely. Anyway, we'll talk. I'll be out to see you tomorrow. For now…well, I've got some crime-scene people taking a look around here. At this point, it looks as if Seth got a bit too tipsy, took a walk, met the water and then his maker. There's going to have to be a hearing, though, and an autopsy. The medical examiner will have to verify that scenario."

Jay nodded glumly. "Still," he murmured, "at least it happened here, not at Moon Bay." The other two looked at him. "Hey, I'm sorry, but it matters."

"Well, take your guests home, Jay," Thompson said. "You." He pointed at Alex. "I'll see you tomorrow."

"Sure," she murmured.

They left, bidding Warren goodbye. Alex hoped the restaurant wouldn't end up paying for Seth's alcohol consumption. She knew Warren usually watched his customers and had been known to confiscate keys from any driver he thought shouldn't be on the road. His staff was equally vigilant.

From what she had seen, there had been a pitcher of beer on the table. Seth had probably been downing pitcher after pitcher himself, but the waitress had undoubtedly assumed the beer was being consumed by a party of five.

As they walked along the deck toward the boat, Jay stopped Alex. "I'll go back on the dive boat," he told her. "Damage control," he said with a wince.

"There's room for us both," she said.

"Take a break. Go back on the *Icarus*," he said. "That's okay with you, right, David?" Jay asked, turning slightly.

She hadn't realized that her ex—or not quite ex—husband had been right behind them. "Sure," he said.

Great. A ride back with David, John Seymore and Hank Adamson.

Still, she didn't want to make a draining evening any worse, so she shrugged. At least the ride wouldn't take long.

Along with a sympathetic smile, John Seymore offered her a hand down into the little dinghy that would take them back to the *Icarus*. She wound up sitting next to Hank Adamson, while David and John had the oars. Once again, it was John who gave her a hand on board the *Icarus*, but once there, she hurried aft, hoping to make the journey back alone.

No luck.

She had barely settled down on the deck, choosing a spot she had often chosen in years past, when David joined her.

She groaned aloud. "Don't you ever go away?"

"I can't. Not now."

She stared at him. "You know, I'm trying to have a relationship with someone else."

"I don't know about him yet."

"What don't you know about him?"

He looked at her, blue eyes coolly touching hers. "I don't know if he's in on what's going on or not."

She groaned again. "David, he hasn't been out of the military that long. He's from the West Coast. He's not into salvage."

"He's into things connected with the sea, that's for certain."

"So?"

"So I still don't know about him."

"How about letting me make a few judgments on my own?"

"Did you see a corpse on the beach or not?" he demanded.

She looked away, silently damning him. "Yes."

"And are we absolutely positive that Seth Granger just got up, left a bar, fell into the water and drowned?"

"No," she admitted after a moment. "But it's the most likely scenario."

"'Most likely' doesn't make it fact," he said flatly. "The body that you found—and yes, I'm convinced you found a body—was Alicia's. I'm certain of it."

"How do you know that?" she demanded, but then she knew. One of his best friends, Dane Whitelaw, worked in Key Largo, leading his version of an ideal life, running a dive service and an investigations business. "Never mind. You've had Dane looking into it."

"Yup."

"So do you understand now?"

"Understand what?"

"Why I need to keep you under my wing for the time being."

"Under your wing?" she snapped.

"Don't get bristly," he protested. "After all, we're still married."

"A technicality."

"Even if we weren't, I'd be damned if I'd allow anyone to hurt you."

"John Seymore doesn't intend to hurt me," she said. Then she couldn't resist adding, "Unless I want him to."

He glared at her, eyes hard. "You just won't take this seriously, will you?"

"How do I know you haven't suddenly turned into a murderer in your quest for treasure?"

"Quit fighting me, please. I really don't want to sleep on your porch tonight. It will just make me harder to get along with. And if I'm cranky, I won't go to see a lawyer with you. And once I find out what's going on here…well, I could just take off again and leave you in limbo for a very long time."

"You wouldn't!" she said.

"I didn't file the papers in the first place," he said with a shrug, then rose. "We're nearly back. I've got to go dock her."

Left alone, Alex felt her temper rising, but she wasn't as furious with him at that moment as she was with herself. She shouldn't be making a terrible problem out of things. Let the idiot sleep on the couch. Under the circumstances, she needed to take everything slow. If John Seymore was really interested in her, he would wait around.

Even with her ex-or-almost-ex-husband in the cottage?

They had docked. She rose slowly, all too aware of why she was so upset. Having David on the couch should be no big deal.

Except she would know he was there. And now, with each passing moment, she was more and more aware of why she had been so attracted to him from the beginning, why she felt a strange flush of excitement when he was around, and why she found herself so annoyed that he ran around shirtless so often.

"We really do need to talk," David murmured as they went ashore, following Hank Adamson and John Seymore off the *Icarus*.

"I really need to see to my dolphins," she told him, and purposely walked as quickly as she could along the docks, aiming straight for the dolphin lagoon and praying, for once, that she wouldn't be followed. By anyone.

"Come to the Tiki Hut with me?" Jay said to David. He'd waited at the end of the deck He was trying to sound casual, but there was an edgy note in his voice.

Damage control, David thought.

"I really need a shower," David told him.

"And I don't think anyone actually wants a drink," Hank Adamson said.

"What the hell, I'll go for a few minutes," John Seymore said.

"We'll all go," David determined. He wanted to keep an eye on the guy. He wasn't sure if he was suspicious because a man like Seymore was in a place like this, or because he was interested in Alex. Interested in her? He'd had his tongue halfway down her throat the other night.

"Apparently the sheriff doesn't believe that Seth Granger just fell in the water and drowned," Hank said as they walked.

"What makes you say that?" Jay asked him sharply.

"He questioned everyone pretty closely."

"He's the sheriff," Jay said uneasily. "He has to cover all bases. Why the hell would anyone want to kill Seth Granger."

The silence that followed his question was telling.

"For being a crass, overbearing windbag, for one," Hank offered dryly.

They reached the Tiki Hut. The employees rushed for Jay as he appeared, and he calmly explained the situation. No one seemed to be terribly sad, David noted. They were amazed, though, and maybe even a little titillated. The drowning of such a wealthy man was bound to excite gossip.

The four men took a table. David admired Jay's determination to deal with the situation. He wanted to be visible, to answer any questions. That was damage control, yes, but at least the guy wasn't shrinking from his responsibility.

Zach's mother, Ally Conroy—the one person who had seemed to be getting on with Seth the night before—was in the bar without her son, and it appeared she'd had a few herself. She rose, walked to the table and demanded, "Are they really saying he just...got up and drowned?"

"That's what they think right now, yes," Jay told her.

"I don't believe it. I didn't know him that well, but I don't believe it," she said, slurring her words. "Everyone was there, right with him. How come no one saw?" Ally demanded. Her voice was strong, but she was shifting from foot to foot as she spoke.

"Probably because none of us was expecting anything to happen," David told her, rising. "Mrs. Conroy, you seem...distraught. Would you like me to walk you to your room?"

"Why? Because I might fall into the water and drown?" she said with hostility.

"Because I wouldn't want you to hurt yourself in any way," David said.

Suddenly her eyes fell. She sniffed. "He liked me. Liked Zach and liked me. You don't know how hard it is to raise a kid by yourself. And he was…not the kind of man who'd get drunk, fall in the water and drown."

"The sheriff will be investigating," David assured her gently. "In fact, he'll be here tomorrow. You can talk to him yourself."

She suddenly seemed to deflate, hanging on David's arm. She looked up at him, a little bleary-eyed. "Hey, you're all right, you know?"

"I'll walk her to her room," David told the others.

They nodded.

Ally Conroy was definitely stumbling as she clung to David. "We've got one of the cottages," she said. "It was an Internet deal. Cool, huh? I'm paying a lot less than most people. Have to watch my money, you know?"

"Of course. I'm glad you got a good deal."

By the time they reached her cottage, he was ready to pick her up and throw her over his shoulder, she was stumbling so badly. He damned himself for taking the time to go with her, was even now missing something being said at the Tiki Hut, some piece of the puzzle that had to come together soon.

Because he didn't believe, not for a minute, that Seth Granger had just fallen into the water and died.

They reached the cottage at last. She couldn't find her key, so David knocked on the door, hoping Zach would hear.

"He was onto something. Onto something big," Ally said suddenly.

"What?"

"He told me about some ship."

"What ship?"

"Where is that damn key?" Ally Conroy said.

David strove for patience and an even tone. "Mrs. Conroy, what ship? Please, think for me."

"The…ship. He was going after a ship. Said he had a friend who needed help, and he intended to help her, because it might be the best thing he'd done in his life. Will you look at this purse? It's an absolute mess."

"Don't worry, there's a key in there somewhere, and if not, Zach will open the door. Mrs. Conroy, you could really help me out here. Did Seth know the name of the ship he wanted to find?"

"The name of the ship…" she repeated.

"The name."

"Oh…yes! The Anne Marie, I think he said." Her eyes brightened, and she smiled, forgetting her quest for her key for a moment. "He was very excited about it. He said there was more fantasy written about her than fact. That the legend had it all wrong. No, history was wrong, legend was right." She shook her head and gave her attention back to her purse. "Where is that damned key?"

The door opened. Zach looked at them anxiously.

"I thought I should walk your mom to your cottage," David said.

Zach looked amazingly world-weary, understanding and tolerant. "Thanks, Mr. Denham."

"No problem, and call me David."

The kid nodded, taking his mother's arm.

"I'm okay," Ally said, steadying herself. She cupped

Zach's face, then gave him a kiss on the forehead. "I guess we have to take care of each other, huh? I'm sorry, hon."

"It's okay, Mom."

"I'm going to lie down," Ally said.

"Good idea," Zach told her.

Ally paused, looking at David. "I...thank you," she said.

"Not at all."

"I'll try to remember anything else I can," she told him. "After an aspirin and a night's sleep," she added dryly.

"Thanks again."

Ally walked inside. Zach looked at David. "She liked Mr. Granger," he said with a shrug. "I was sorry, but...I didn't want her getting all tied up with him. I know she was thinking it would be great for me to have a dad, but he was a loudmouth. And rude. I didn't want my mom with him. I didn't make him fall in the water, though."

"I never thought you did, Zach," David said.

"Thanks," Zach said. As David started to walk away, he called him back. "Hey, Mr. Denham? David?"

"Yes?"

"Maybe sometime, if you're not too busy, you could show me the *Icarus*?"

"I'd be glad to," David said. "Maybe tomorrow. Ask your Mom. Maybe we can have coffee together, or breakfast, and I'll take you both out on her."

In all honesty, he liked the kid. Especially after tonight.

And he damn sure wanted to talk to Ally Conroy when she was sober.

Before anyone else did.

Chapter 7

Len Creighton was off work, and he considered his free time as totally his own. He sat nursing a double stinger at the Tiki Hut. He needed it.

He'd been behind the desk when a news brief had interrupted the television program in the lobby with the stunning information that millionaire tycoon Seth Granger was dead, apparently by drowning. There was little other information at the time, but he'd heard more about it once the boats had returned to Moon Bay. It had been pretty much the only topic of conversation in the Tiki Hut.

He was still hearing the buzz about it from other tables when Hank Adamson sat down in front of him.

"Long day, huh?" Adamson said, indicating Len's drink.

"Longer for you, I imagine, Mr. Adamson."

"You can call me Hank, please. Yeah, we were there a long time. The sheriff asked everyone if anyone had seen Seth go out or fall in the water. No one had."

"No one saw him? How sad," Len said.

Hank lifted a hand to order a drink. After giving his order, he told Len, "Sad thing is, I don't think anyone cared."

"I care," Len said in protest. He shrugged sheepishly. "He always tipped well."

"He was rude as hell to the waitress today. You don't think she pushed him into the drink, do you?"

Len smiled, but knew he had to be careful with Hank Adamson. "I'm sure he was just tipsy and fell in himself."

"That old sheriff…he's something, though. Ever had a homicide in this area?"

"Not since I've been here."

"Well, there you go. A local-yokel sheriff just trying to make a name for himself."

"Nigel's a good guy," Len defended.

"So you think he really thinks there was foul play?" Hank asked, smiling at the waitress and accepting a beer from her.

"He's no yokel," Len said.

Adamson leaned toward him. "Why would someone murder Granger? They aren't going to be blaming it on any ex-wife. If he was killed, it had to be someone who was with us at that bar. Someone on the staff at Moon Bay?"

"No way!" Len protested.

"Your boss admits he wants in on a lot of action," Hank said. "He'd love to get into the salvage operations business."

Len stood up. Writer or no, Hank Adamson had crossed the line.

"Jay is as honest as the day is long," Len said firmly.

"Hey, an honest man can be driven to murder," Hank said, smiling as he took another sip of beer straight from the bottle. "Sit down. I like your boss. In my opinion, the jerk just fell off the pier. Finish your drink, and I'll buy you another."

Len hesitated. Then, looking across the dance floor, he noticed Jay, who saw him, and motioned that he'd be over momentarily.

Len smiled. "Jay will be joining us in just a minute," he told Hank. He sipped his drink, then was embarrassed to experience a huge yawn before he could suppress it. "Sorry. It's been a long day."

"Way too long. I don't guess many of us will be hanging around here too late tonight," Hank said.

A few minutes later, when Jay came over, Len rose, stifling another yawn, and bade the two good-night.

There was no sign of Laurie Smith at the lagoons, but she wasn't required to be there—it was her day off, for one thing. Still, Alex was surprised. Laurie really loved the dolphins and tried to spend time with them every day.

She hesitated, then pulled out her cell phone and tried Laurie's room. There was no answer. She dialed Laurie's cell-phone number next, but got voice mail.

Strange.

Mandy and Gil were both there, though. They'd already heard what had happened but she gave them the full story of how she'd found him.

"Man, imagine that. A guy can have everything in the

world, and still..." Gil said, shaking his head. "Just last night, he was flirting and drinking half the beer in the place. He had one hell of a capacity for liquor."

"I guess so. That seems to be what everyone says," Alex said.

"Tragic when anyone dies like that," Mandy said, shaking his dark head. "He was coming on to that Ally woman last night, and she was eating it up. He was boasting about something really big he was into. I thought the guy was a jerk, myself."

"Hank Adamson was there when it happened, right?" Gil said, rolling his eyes.

"He was there. One of the last to see him alive," Alex said.

"Bet he'll love telling that story," Gil said. "Anyway, I know you want to hear about these guys," he told her, indicating the dolphins.

Mandy showed her the log book for the day. "We were bringing them their good-night snack," Gil said. "Didn't know when you'd be back. But you can take over."

"That's all right," she said.

Mandy laughed. "No, it's not. We know you like to tuck them in."

She smiled. "You two do fine without me," Alex said.

"Hell, the swim was a piece of cake next to your day," Mandy said. "Seth Granger dead. Go figure." He made a face. "And you found him floating. I'm glad it wasn't me."

"You look all done in. We'll take off and leave you to your babies," Gil said. "I'm sure you don't want to replay the afternoon anymore."

"It's okay, but you're right. Truthfully, I don't want to talk about it anymore. Not now, anyway," she agreed.

"Good night, then," Gil said.

"Hey, wait!" she called. They stopped, looking at her expectantly. "Has either of you seen Laurie today?" she asked.

"I haven't," Gil said, looking at Mandy.

"I haven't either. But it is her day off," Mandy said.

"I haven't seen her since last night. She left the Tiki Hut kind of late. She'd been talking to Hank Adamson. She was holding her own against him, too, and the guy can be a real pain," Gil said.

"Yeah, he can. Did he grill either of you?" Alex asked.

"Nope," Gil said. "I was at the Tiki Hut after she left, but…I don't remember seeing Adamson after that, either, actually. But hey, I'm a bald guy with a gold earring, and Laurie is a cute girl. I'd grill her, too, if I were Adamson." He frowned suddenly. "Are you worried about her?"

"No. Not really. It's her day off. She's free to come and go as she pleases," Alex said.

"Actually, come to think of it, Len was looking for her earlier, too," Mandy said.

"Why?"

"I think he had mail for her. Or maybe he just knew that she'd been talking to Hank Adamson, and wanted to make sure she hadn't said anything she shouldn't." He shrugged.

Gil let out a snort. "Adamson is going to write what he wants, no matter what any of us say. Only thing is, now he's going to have an awful lot more to write about, having been there when Seth Granger bit the big one."

"Gil…" Alex said with a groan.

"I'll take a walk by Laurie's room and knock," Gil said. "But maybe she just doesn't want to be disturbed."

"Yeah. She could have a hot date," Mandy agreed.

"You think?" Alex said. She shook her head. "She would have told me. She hated that Date Tournament thing she went on."

"Yeah, but...she sure was impressed by your ex-husband," Mandy said.

"And the blond guy chasing you around the last few days," Gil commented.

"Well, they were both there today when Seth—as you so gently put it—bit the big one," Alex said.

"I'm sure she's fine," Gil said. "I'm sure she'll turn up by morning. Maybe she's somewhere right now, hearing all about Seth Granger. Jay must be having fits. That kind of publicity, connected to his precious Moon Bay."

"Haven't you heard? There's no such thing as bad publicity. We'll probably get more people hanging around. In another year, Warren will be advertising that he has a ghost," Mandy said.

"Hey, the guy is barely cold!" Alex protested.

"Sorry," Mandy told her.

"Let's get out of here and let the boss have her private time," Gil said to him. "Night, Alex."

The two walked off. Alex suddenly felt very alone.

For a moment she felt a chill, but then realized that the Tiki Hut was blazing with light and music, and she was just across the lagoon from it. She didn't need to feel alone or afraid, she assured herself. And she wouldn't.

The time was now. And there wouldn't be much of it.

Using the pass key he'd obtained, he slipped it into the front door of the cottage, quickly closing it behind him, then locking it again.

If someone should arrive, there was always the back door.

Where to look…?

The bedroom. He'd been there before.

He went straight for the dresser, staring at the things on top of it. He picked up the dolphin again, studying it, shaking it. Perfume sprayed out at him. Choking, he put it down.

There was a beautiful painting of a dolphin on the wall. He walked over to it, lifted it from its hook, returned it.

Anger filled him. He didn't have enough information, and despite all he'd done, he couldn't get it. Hell, everywhere he looked, there were dolphins around this woman. Live ones, stuffed ones, ceramic ones.

He heard footsteps coming toward the cottage and hurried for the back door. As long as he wasn't caught, he could come back and take all the time he wanted to study every dolphin in the place.

And he wasn't going to be caught. He would made sure of that this time.

Outside the cottage, he swore. He could have had more time right then. It was just one of the damn maids, walking down the trail.

He smiled at her, waved and kept going.

Back toward the lights and the few people still milling around at the Tiki Hut.

David's phone rang as he headed back along the path. When he saw Dane Whitelaw's name flash on the ID screen, he paused, taking the call.

"What did you find out?"

"I'm fine, thanks," Dane said dryly. "How are you?"

David paused. "Sorry, how are you? The cat, the dog? Wife, kids...the tropical fish?"

Dane laughed on the other end. "I researched your navy boy. Seems he's telling you the truth. He left the military a year ago May. Was married to a Serena Anne Franklin, no kids. They split up right about the time he left the service. He's in business for himself, incorporated as Seymore Consultants—there are no other consultants listed, however. There is one interesting thing. He was in Miami for a month before coming down here."

"So...it's possible he met up with Alicia Farr there?"

"It's possible, but there are millions of people in the area."

"Great. The guy may be legit—and may not be."

"I'll tell you one thing, he has degrees up the kazoo. Engineering, psychology, geography, with a minor in oceanography."

"Don't you just hate an underachiever?" David muttered.

"Bet the guy made a lot of contacts over the years. Men in high places. Foreign interests, too, I imagine."

"So just what are you saying? Does that clear him, or make him more suspicious?" David asked.

"In a case like this, I can tell you what I'd go by. Gut instinct."

"What does your gut instinct say?" David asked.

"Nothing. You have to go by your own gut instinct. You know him. I don't. Hey, by the way. I see it's getting even more tangled down there. I saw it on the news."

"Seth Granger?"

"You bet. Millionaire drowns and it's on every channel in the state. What happened? What aren't they saying?"

"I don't know."

"You were there."

"I was talking to you when he walked out and went swimming."

"Curious, isn't it? A guy who could—and would—have financed the whole thing goes down."

"Yeah, curious," David agreed, then added slowly, "Unless someone knows more than we do."

"Like what?"

"Like the ship being somewhere easy to reach. Where someone in a little boat could take a dive down and get a piece of the treasure before the heavy equipment—and the government—moved in. For someone who isn't a millionaire, grabbing a few pretty pieces worth hundreds of thousands before the real discovery was made could be an enticing gamble."

"You might be on to something," Dane agreed. "I'll keep digging on your navy man. Keep mc posted. And be careful. There's a storm out there, you know."

"Small one, heading the other way, right?"

"Who knows? Small, yes, but still tropical-storm status. And they think it might turn and hit they Keys after all. Anyway, give a ring if you need anything else."

"Thanks."

David closed the phone, sliding it back into his pocket. The tangles were definitely intensifying. And there was only one person he could really clear in Alicia's disappearance and probable death.

Seth Granger.

Who was now among the departed himself.

Hearing a rustling in the trees, he turned, a sharp frown creasing his forehead. Long strides took him straight into the brush.

There was no one there.

But had there been? Someone who had been walking along, heard his phone ring…

And paused to listen in on the conversation?

Alex sat at the edge of the first platform with her bucket of fish and called out, though she knew the dolphins were already aware she was there. "Katy, Sabra, Jamie Boy!"

They popped up almost instantly, right at her dangling feet. They knew the time of day and knew when they got treats. She stroked them one by one, talking to them, giving them their fish. Then she moved on to the next lagoon and the platform that extended into it. "Shania, get up here," she said. "You, too, Sam, Vicky."

She gave them all the same attention, her fingers lingering just a shade longer on Shania's sleek body. The dolphin watched her with eyes that were almost eerily wise. "You're my children, you know that, guys? Maybe I shouldn't be quite so attached, but, hey…when I had a guy, he was at sea all the time anyway."

"Was he?" The sound of David's voice was so startling, she nearly threw her bucket into the lagoon.

She leaped up and spun around. "Must you sneak up on people?"

"I didn't sneak up, I walked," he told her.

"You scared me to death."

"Didn't mean to. Still, I couldn't help hearing what you said. So…was that it? I was away too much?"

"David, there wasn't one 'it.' My decision to ask for a divorce was complicated. Based on a number of things."

"Was one of them Alicia."

"No. Yes. Maybe. I don't even know anymore, David."

"I asked you to go on every expedition I took," he said.

"But I work with dolphins. They know when I'm gone."

"So you can never go anywhere?"

"I didn't say that. I just can't pick up and leave constantly. And I don't want to. I like a trip as much as the next person, but I like having a home, too."

"You had a home."

"We had a series of apartments. Several in one year. There was always a place that seemed more convenient. For you."

He was silent for a minute, then asked, "Was I really that bad?"

"Yes. No. Well, you're you. You shouldn't have changed what you were—are—for me. Or anyone else. It just didn't work for me."

"There is such a thing as compromise," he reminded her.

"Well, I didn't particularly want to be the reason the great David Denham missed out on the find of the century."

"There are many finds—every century," he told her. "Are you through here? I came to walk back to the cottage with you."

"What makes you think I don't have other plans?" she demanded.

He grinned. "I know you. There's nothing you adore

more than the sea—and your children here, of course—but you're also determined on showering the minute you're done with it."

"Fine. Walk me back, then. I definitely don't want to get dragged into the Tiki Bar," she said wearily, aware that she no longer felt alone—or afraid.

"Want me to take the bucket?"

"Wait—there's one more round for these three."

"May I?" he asked.

She shrugged. David sat on the dock. As she had, he talked to each of the dolphins as he rewarded them with their fish. Spoke, stroked.

She was irrationally irritated that they seemed to like David so much. Only Shania hung back just a little. It was as if she sensed Alex's mixed feelings about him and was awaiting her approval.

David had a knack for speaking with the animals. He understood that food wasn't their only reward, and that they liked human contact, human voices.

Shania, like the others, began to nudge him, asking for attention.

Traitor, Alex thought, but at the same time, she was glad. Shania was a very special creature. She needed more than the others, who had never known the kind of injury and pain that Shania had suffered.

When the dolphins had finished their fish, Alex started down the dock. He walked along with her in silence. She moved fast, trying to keep a bit ahead. No way. He had very long legs.

"If you're trying to run away, it's rather futile, don't you think?"

She stopped short. "Why would I be running away?"

"Because you're hoping to lose me?"

"How can I lose you? We're on a very small island, in case you hadn't noticed."

"Not to mention that my legs are longer, so I can actually leave you in the dust at any time."

"Go ahead."

"You have the key."

"You have your own place here."

"But I'm not leaving you alone in yours."

His tone had been light and bantering, but the last was said with deadly gravity.

"This is insane," she murmured, and hurried on. She knew, though, that she wasn't going to lose him. And in a secret part of herself—physical, surely, not emotional—she felt the birth of a certain wild elation. Why? Did she think she could just play with him? Hope to tempt and tease, then hurt…?

As she felt she had been hurt?

No, surely not. Her decision to file the papers hadn't been based on a fit of temper. She had thought long and hard about every aspect of their lives.

But wasn't it true, an inner voice whispered, that jealousy had played a part? Jealousy, and the fear that others offered more than she ever could, so she couldn't possibly hope to keep him?

Despite his long legs, she sprinted ahead of him as they neared the cottage. She opened the door, ignoring him. She didn't slam it, just let it fall shut. He caught it, though, and followed her in.

Inside, she curtly told him to help himself to the bath in the hallway, then walked into her own room. She stripped right in the shower, then turned the water on hard, sudsing both her hair and body with a vengeance. Finally she got out, wrapped herself in a towel and remembered that the maid never left anything but hand towels in the guest bath.

Cursing at herself, she gathered up one of the big bath sheets and walked into the hallway. He was already in the shower. She tapped on the door. No answer.

"David?"

"What?" he called over the water.

"Here's your towel."

"What? Can't hear you."

Why was she bothering? She should let him drip dry. No, knowing David, he'd just come out in the buff, dripping all over the polished wood floors.

"Your towel!" she shouted.

"Can't hear you!" he responded again.

Impatiently, she tried the door. It was unlocked. She pushed it open, ready to throw the towel right in.

The glass shower door was clear, and the steam hadn't fogged it yet. She was staring right at him, in all his naked glory.

"Your towel," she said, dropping it, ready to run.

The glass door opened, and his head appeared. He was smiling. "Just couldn't resist a look at the old buns, huh?" he teased. "Careful, or you'll be too tempted to resist."

She forced herself to stand dead still, slowly taking stock of him, inch by inch. She kept her gaze entirely impassive. Then, her careful scrutiny complete, she spoke at last.

"No," she said, and with a casual turn, exited the bathroom. She heard his throaty laughter and leaned against the closed door, feeling absurdly weak. Damn him. Every sinewy, muscle-bound bit of him. But as she closed her eyes, it wasn't just the sleek bronze vision of his flesh that taunted her.

It was all the ways he could use it.

The door opened suddenly, giving way to her weight as she leaned against it. She fell backward, right into his very damp, very warm and very powerful arms.

Chapter 8

It probably wasn't strange that he refused to release her instantly.

"You were spying on me!" he said.

"Spying—through a closed door?" she returned.

"You were listening at the door."

"I wasn't," she assured him. His arms were wrapped around her midriff, and they were both wearing nothing but towels. "I was leaning against it."

"Weakened by the sight of me, right?" he whispered huskily, the sound just against her ear and somehow leaving a touch that seemed to seep down the length of her neck, spread into a radiance of sun warmth and radiate along the length of her.

"I divorced you, remember?" she said softly.

"I've never forgotten. Not for an instant." There was

something haunting in his voice, and his hold hadn't eased in the least.

"Would you please let me go?"

"Damn. You're not charmed, standing there, me here, my body, your body…memories."

She fought very hard not to move an inch, certain he was just taunting her, and afraid she was feeling so much more than she should.

"I never denied that you could be incredibly charming," she said, trying for calm, as if she were dealing with a child. "When you chose."

"I'm choosing now."

"Too late."

"Why? We're still technically married, remember? Here we are…together, you know I won't leave this cottage, and I think you believe my concern for you is real. And you are my wife."

In a minute she would melt. She might even burst into tears. Worse, she might turn around and throw herself into his arms, then cry out all her insecurities and her belief that they'd never had a chance of making it.

"David, let me go," she said.

"Whatever you wish." He released her. The minute he did, she lost her towel.

She turned to face him, deciding not to make a desperate grab for it. Standing as casual and tall as she could, she shook her head. "That was a rather childish trick."

"It wasn't a trick. I let you go and your towel fell off. Not my fault."

"Well, thank God you still have yours."

He grinned and dropped his towel. And his smile, as well.

For a moment he stood there, watching her, with no apology at all for the visible extent of his arousal.

He took a step toward her, reaching for her, pulling her into his arms, hard and flush against his length. She knew, though, that if she protested with even a word or a gesture, he would let her go again.

She meant to say…something.

But she didn't. His fingers brushed her chin, lifting her face, tilting her head. Neither of them spoke. His eyes searched hers for a moment; then his mouth met her lips with an onslaught that was forceful, staggering. It took only the touch of his lips, the thrust of his tongue, the simple vibrant crush of his body, and she felt the stirring of sexual tension within her so deeply that she thought she would scream. If he had lowered her to the tile floor then and there, she wouldn't have thought of denial.

But he did no such thing. His lips and tongue met hers with a flattering urgency, and his hands moved down the length of her back, fingers brushing slowly, until they had cleared the base of her spine, curved around her buttocks and pressed her closer still. She felt the hard crush of his erection against her inner thighs, equal parts threat and promise, a pulsing within, creating a swirl of pure sensuality that possessed some core within her. Weakened, shaking, she clung to him, still intoxicated by the movements of his lips, teeth and tongue.

And his hands, of course, pressing, caressing…

She drew away as his lips broke from hers. She needed to say something. Married or not, they shouldn't be here now. She had moved on. For the first time she had felt chemistry with another man. With…

She couldn't even recall his name.

David's mouth had broken from hers, only to settle on her collarbone, where his tongue drew heated circles, then move lower.

"David," she breathed. He didn't answer, because the fiery warmth of his caress had traveled to the valley between her breasts, and with each brush of flesh, she felt the need for the teasing to stop, for his lips to settle, for his body to…

"David…"

Her fingers were digging into his shoulder then. His tongue bathed her flesh, erasing any little drops that remained from her shower. Everywhere a slow, languid, perhaps even studied caress, everywhere, until thosc areas he did not touch burned with aching anticipation. Her abdomen was laved, thighs caressed, hips, the hollows behind her knees, her thighs…close…closer….

"David…"

"What?" he murmured at last, rising to his full height, still flush against her, yet meeting her eyes. "Don't tell me to stop," he said, gaze dark and volatile, "Alex, don't tell me to stop."

"I—I wasn't going to," she stuttered.

He arched an eyebrow.

"I was going to tell you that I couldn't stand, that…I was about to fall."

"Ah," he murmured, watching her for the longest moment as heat and cold seared through her, heat that he held her still, cold, the fear that had come before, that he would leave her, that her life, like her body, would be empty.

"I—I don't think I can stand," she said, swallowing, lashes falling.

"You don't need to," he said, and he swept her up, his arms firm and strong, his eyes a shade of cobalt so dark they might have been pure ebony. He moved the few steps through the hall, eyes upon her all the while, pressed open the bedroom door and carried her in. And still he watched her, and in the long gaze he gave her, she felt the stirring in her quicken to a deeper hunger, urgency, desperation. It was almost as if he could physically stroke her with that gaze, touch every erogenous zone, reach inside her, caress her very essence.

She breathed his name again. "David."

At last he set her down, and though she longed just to circle her arms around him, feel him inside her, he had no such quick intent. He captured her mouth again, kissed her with a hot, openmouthed passion that left her breathless. And while she sought air in the wake of his tempest, he moved against her again, mouth capturing her breasts, tending to each with fierce urgency. She felt the hardness of her own nipples, felt them peaking against his mouth and tongue, and then the cold of the air struck them and brought shivers as he moved his body against hers. This time he didn't tease, but parted her thighs and used his mouth to make love to her with a shocking, vital intimacy, until she no longer arched and whispered his name, but writhed with abandon and desperation, unable to get close enough, unable to free herself, ravenous for more and more.

Sweet familiarity. He knew her. Knew how to make love to her. Time had taught him to play her flesh and soul, and he gave no quarter, ignored the hammering in his own head, the frantic pulse in his blood, a drumbeat she could feel against her limbs. She cried out at last, stunned, swept away, crashing upon a wave of physical ecstasy so sweet it left her breathless once again, almost numb, the beat of her own heart loud in ears. But before she could drift magically back down to the plane of real existence, he was with her, as she had craved, body thrusting into hers, their limbs entangled. The roller coaster began a fierce climb once again, driving upward with a frenetic volatility that made all the world disappear and, in time, explode once again in a sea of sheer sensual splendor, so violent in its power that she saw nothing but black, then stars…then, at last, the bedroom again, and the man still wrapping her with his arms. Shudders continued to ripple through her, little after currents of electricity, and as they brought her downward, she couldn't help but marvel at the sheer sexual prowess of the man and the almost painful chemistry they shared.

He rose up on his elbow, slightly above her, and used his free hand to smooth a straying lock of damp hair from her face. She was startled to see the tension that remained in his eyes as he studied her. And she was more startled still by the husky tone in his voice when he suddenly demanded, "Why?"

"Why?" she repeated.

"Why did you do it? You didn't call…you didn't write. You sent divorce papers."

She stared back at him. Why?

Because I couldn't bear the thought of you having this with any other woman—ever. Because I was losing you. Losing myself. I was happy at your side, but I needed my own world, as well. And I was sure that one day you would realize I wasn't the kind of woman you could spend forever with.

She didn't speak the words. It wasn't the time. She was far too off balance. She moistened her lips, desperately seeking for something to say.

"Sex doesn't make a marriage," she managed at last. He frowned slightly, staring at her still.

She pushed him away from her. "David…you're heavy," she said, though it wasn't true.

But he shifted off her. She rose and sped into her bathroom, where she just closed the door and stood there, shivering. Finally she turned the shower on and stepped beneath it. If they had really still been married, he would have followed her. He could do absolutely incredible things with a soap bar in his hands, with suds, with water, with teasing, laughing, growing serious all over again, heated….

He didn't follow her. She didn't know how long she stayed in the shower, but when she emerged, he had left her bedroom.

She found a long sleep shirt and slipped into it, then paused to brush out the length of her now twice-washed hair. She realized that she was starving, yet opted not to leave her room.

She set the brush back down on her dresser and noted that her array of toiletries was out of order. The women in housekeeping never touched her dresser, which she kept in order herself, or her desk and computer, in the spare bedroom. Had David been going through her things?

She had a dolphin perfume dispenser. It wasn't valuable, but it was pretty and meant a lot to her, because her parents had given it to her for her tenth birthday. It was porcelain, about five inches high and beautifully painted. She always set it in the middle and arranged the rest of her toiletries around it. Now the dolphin was off to the side and a fancy designer fragrance was in the center. By rote, she rearranged the perfumes, talcs and lotions.

No big deal. Just…curious.

She shrugged, still thinking about making love with David. One part of her wondered how the hell she had lived without him, without being together like that, for an entire year. The other part of her was busy calling herself the worst kind of fool in the world.

Then she reminded herself that she shouldn't be dwelling on personal considerations at all. A man had died today. This time there was no doubt that she had found a body.

In her own mind—and, apparently, in David's—there was no doubt that she had found a body on the beach, as well. And in David's mind, that body had belonged to Alicia Farr. His friend? His sometime lover? Either way, it had to disturb him deeply, and yet…

And yet, there they had been tonight.

She set her brush down, completely forgetting that the toiletries on her dresser had been rearranged.

Then she crawled into bed. Somchow, she was going to make herself sleep.

Alone.

She really could look like an angel, David thought, opening the door to her bedroom. She was sound asleep in a cloud of sun-blond hair, her hand lying on the pillow beside her face. Just seeing her like that, he felt both a swelling of tenderness…and a stirring of desire.

Determinedly, he tampered down both.

He had the coffee going; he'd returned to his own place in a flash for clothing, and then put out cereal and fruit for breakfast. He hadn't forgotten that he'd promised Zach that he would show him—and his mother—the *Icarus*, and mentioned to the boy that they might meet for breakfast, but it was too early to meet them, and if Alex had maintained her old habits, she would forget to eat during the day, so she needed to start out with something.

And he needed to talk with her.

He walked into the room, ripping the covers from her and giving her shoulder a firm shake. She awoke instantly and irritably, glaring at him as if she were the crown princess, and he a lowly serf who had dared disturb her.

"Breakfast," he said briefly.

She glanced at her alarm. "I don't have to be up yet," she told him indignantly.

"Yes, you do."

"No, I don't."

"Trust me, you do."

She groaned, resting her head in her hands. "Really, David, this is getting to be too much. Listen, last night was…nothing but the spur of the moment. You need an ego boost? It was just the fact that you do have nice buns and you've managed to ruin my one chance for a nice affair here. At any rate, you can stay here if you want to, so knock yourself out. But I've just about had it with you acting like a dictator."

"Then maybe you should quit lying to me."

"About what?" she demanded, looking outraged.

"Danny Fuller."

She groaned. "Now I really don't know what you're talking about."

"Get up. There's coffee. That always seems to improve your temper."

"I don't have a temper."

"I beg to differ," he told her, and added, "Come on, out here, and you can eat while you talk."

He didn't let her answer but exited the room. Just after he had closed the door, he heard the pillow crash against it.

He turned and opened it. "No temper, huh?" he queried.

She still wasn't up. Tangled blond hair was all around her face, and she was in a soft cotton T-shirt that didn't do a thing to make her any less appealing. It should have been loose, but somehow it managed only to enhance her curves.

He closed the door quickly before she could find something else to throw.

In the kitchen, he poured two cups of coffee, then hesitated where he stood, tension gripping his abdomen in a hard spasm.

What the hell had gone so wrong between them? He'd never met anyone like her. He loved everything about her, from her eyes to her toes, the sound of her voice, her passion when she spoke about dolphins, teaching, the sea, and the way she looked when they made love, the way she moved, touched him, the smell of her, sight, sound, taste….

He'd never fallen out of love with her. When he'd received the divorce papers, he'd been stunned. She hadn't said a word. But it was what she had wanted, so, bitterly, silently, he had given it to her.

He started, putting the coffeepot back as she stumbled into the kitchen, casting him a venomous gaze and reaching for the coffee he had poured for her. She took a seat on one of the counter bar stools, arched an eyebrow to him and poured cereal into a bowl and added milk.

"All right, let's get to it. What was my relationship with Danny Fuller supposed to have been? Did I have a thing going with the old guy or something?"

"Don't be flippant."

"I don't know what the hell else you want me to be. Of all the stuff you've come up with since you've been here, this is the most ridiculous. I don't know what you're talking about."

"All right, I'll tell you. Alicia Farr spent all the time she could with Danny Fuller during his last days at the hospital. And in their conversations, two things kept coming up, dolphins—and your name."

She stared at him. He couldn't believe she had been hiding anything, not the way she was looking at him.

She shook her head at last. "Danny Fuller came here, yes. I liked him. He really liked dolphins, and you know me, I like anyone who likes my dolphins. Sometimes we talked casually in the Tiki Hut. He told me about some of his adventures, but if there was something he wanted to do but never attempted, I swear to you, I don't have the faintest idea what it was."

"Did he ever mention a ship called the Anne Marie to you?"

Staring at him, she gave it a moment's thought, then shook her head slowly. "No. He never mentioned it, and I never heard any stories about a ship named the Anne Marie from anyone else."

David lowered his head. Too bad. It would have helped if Alex had known something.

He gazed up at her again thoughtfully. Either she really didn't know anything or she had added acting to her repertoire of talents. Which might be the case. He had just about forced his presence here. And last night…

Well, according to her, it had been the situation, nothing more. Too many days spent on an island.

"So?" she said. "Is that all you wanted? Is that why you were so insistent on 'protecting' me? If so, honest to God, I can't help you."

"No. You're in danger. If two corpses haven't proven it to you, nothing will."

Her eyes narrowed. "Forget that. You, apparently, have heard about a ship called the Anne Marie."

"Yes."

"Well?"

"She was an English ship that went down in the dying days of the pirate era, in 1715. Records have her sinking off the coast of South Carolina. But the story of her sinking was told by a pirate named Billy Thornton—a pirate who apparently expected a reprieve and didn't get one. As he was about to be hanged, he shouted out, 'She didn't really—'"

"She didn't really what?" Alex demanded.

"Well, people have mused that he was about to say she didn't really go down anywhere near South Carolina. You see, before he was caught, he claimed to have seen the ship go down in a storm that ravaged the Eastern Seaboard, but some historians believe he attacked the ship himself."

"He couldn't have attacked the ship alone," Alex pointed out.

"Some legends suggest that since he was off the Florida coast, it would have been easy for him to go ashore, and kill his own men with the intent of going back himself for the treasure."

"And what was the treasure?" Alex demanded.

"There are full records in the English archives somewhere," he said, "but basically, tons of gold buillion, and a cache of precious gems that would be worth millions today."

Alex shook her head. "I don't understand. There must be hundreds of ships with treasures that sank in the Atlantic and are still out there to be found. Why would people kill over this one?"

"Most people wouldn't kill over any treasure. But the bounty to be found on this particular ship would be just about priceless."

"Did Alicia think she knew where to find the Anne Marie? If so, she should have announced an expedition and gathered people around her. No matter what, she'd have to go by the laws of salvage."

"Yes. But she was afraid, I think, of letting out what she knew. Afraid that someone would beat her to it."

"Why would Danny Fuller have hidden whatever information he had for so many years? If he knew something, why wouldn't he have gone after it himself?"

"I wondered about that myself. Maybe he just found out. It's my assumption that Alicia learned something from Danny Fuller about where the Anne Marie went down. She intended to set up an expedition, and that's why she wanted to meet me here. But she must have talked to other people, as well. And I think someone she brought in on her secret decided that they wanted the secret—and the treasure—for themselves."

"The thing is," David said, hoping he was making an impact on her, "someone is willing to kill for that treasure. And I don't think this person wants the government involved in any way. If he—or she—thinks he can bring up a fortune without the authorities getting wind of it, then I'm assuming whatever information Danny Fuller had, suggested the vessel went down in shallow waters, and that the tides and sand have obscured her. You know, kind of like time itself playing a joke, hiding her in plain sight."

"So...you believe Seth Granger was involved—invited here to meet Alicia, too, and that he didn't just drown, but was killed?" Alex asked.

"It's a possibility," he said. "A probability," he amended.

"How? He was in the bar with everyone else. And he'd clearly been drinking too much. And if someone did kill Alicia, and it was her body that I found...how in the hell did it just disappear?"

"Obviously it was moved."

"Have you talked to Sheriff Thompson about this?"

"Not directly. I haven't had a chance. I had Dane call him, though, and give him all the information he acquired when I asked him to check into things."

"Great," Alex murmured. "Do you have any idea who this person is?"

"Someone with an interest in the sea and salvage. I

thought at first that it might have been Seth, but now…apparently not."

"Who else might Alicia have invited here?" Alex asked. "Or who else might have gotten wind of what was going on?"

"Well, Seth was rich—he could have provided the funding she would need for the expedition. She invited me for my expertise. I'm not sure who else she might have invited."

"So who might have found out something?"

"Your boss, for one."

"Jay? But he isn't an expert salvage diver. As far as I know, he's competent enough on a boat, but he doesn't have the kind of money you'd need for an expedition like this and…" She paused and shrugged. "I see. You think he'd like to have that kind of money. And he would love to be respected for a discovery of that kind." She shook her head. "I can't believe it. Not Jay."

"There's Hank Adamson," David said.

She stared at him incredulously. "He's a reporter."

"And he's very conveniently here right now."

"I think you're reaching," she said.

"Maybe."

"Is there anyone else on your list of suspects?" she asked.

"Just one."

"Who?"

He hesitated before answering. "Your ex–navy SEAL," he told her quietly.

She rose, pushing her cereal bowl away. "I have to go to work," she said curtly, turning her back on him.

He went after her, catching her arm, turning her

around to face him. "Please, Alex. Honestly, I'm not trying to run your life, much less ruin it, but for now…just until we get to the bottom of this, don't be alone with anyone, okay?"

"Except for you?" she asked, and her tone was dry.

"Except for me, yes," he said flatly.

She tried to pull away.

"Alex, please?"

"I have to go to work, David," she said, staring at his fingers where they wrapped around her arm. She met his eyes as he let her go and added bitterly, "You really don't have anything to worry about. Last night might have been…unintended, but still, I'd never switch around between men with that kind of speed. I like John, yes. I admire him, and I certainly enjoy his company. But I have a few things to settle with myself before… Under the circumstances—let's see, those being that we're not legally divorced and we may have two murders on our hands—I'll be taking my time getting to know anyone. Will that do?"

He hated the way her eyes were sharp and cold as they touched his. But she had given him the answer he needed from her. He nodded. She turned and headed for the bedroom, and a few minutes later, wearing the simple outfit she wore to work with the dolphins, she came back out, heading straight for the door.

She turned back and said, "Don't forget to lock up when you leave." A slight frown creased her forehead.

"What is it?"

"Nothing. Just don't forget to lock up before you leave. My keys are by the door. Please make sure you pick them up."

She walked out, and he felt as if an icy blast passed by.

Alex's actual degree had been in psychology, with a minor in marine sciences. But as far as her work went, she had learned more from an old trainer when she had interned in the center of the state. He had pointed out to her that the same theories that worked with people also worked with animals. Most animals, like most people, responded best to a reward system.

With dolphins, a reward didn't have to be fish. Like people, they craved affection.

Take Shania. She accepted fish and certainly had a healthy appetite. But she also seemed to know that her vets and the workers here had given her life back to her. The best reward for her came from free swims with the people she loved, mainly Alex and Gil. That morning, after feeding her charges with Gil, Alex entered the lagoon with them, one at a time, for a play period.

At eight, an hour before the first swim was due to begin, there was still no sign of Laurie Smith. Concerned, she called Laurie's cottage, then her cell phone, and received only her voice mail. Worried then, she called Jay.

"I don't know where Laurie is," she told him. "She isn't here, and she isn't answering her phone."

"Give her fifteen minutes, then we'll start a search. She's been talking about taking a few days to visit her family in St. Augustine, but I can't believe she'd just leave without asking for the time. Unless…she's just walking out on us," Jay said over the phone.

"She loves her job. She wouldn't just walk out," Alex told him.

"I'll send someone around to her cottage," Jay promised. “By the way, we may be evacuating our guests and the majority of our personnel soon.”

“Evacuating?” she said, stunned.

“Don’t you ever watch television?”

“Sorry, I just haven’t seen the news lately,” she murmured.

“That storm stalled. The forecasters still believe she’s heading for the Carolinas, but at the moment she’s standing her ground. She’s still not a monster storm, and this place is equipped with an emergency generator, but we can’t keep the whole place running if we lose electricity and water. We’ll move everyone inland for a few days if the storm doesn’t take the swing she’s supposed to by tomorrow. Along with most of the staff.”

Alex hesitated. “I’m not leaving,” she said, and added a hopeful, “Am I?”

She heard his sigh. “No, Alex, if it’s your choice, you get to stay.”

“Thanks.”

“You know a lot of people would want to be out of here in the blink of an eye,” he cautioned.

“This place has weathered a few storms already. The storm room is perfectly safe.”

“I knew you wouldn’t leave your dolphins unless someone dragged you off,” Jay said. “All right, let me go. I’ll get someone out to check on Laurie.”

“Thanks.”

Alex returned to the main platform area, where all guests met before breaking into two parties, no more than eight swimmers in each lagoon. Guests began to trickle in to get flippers and masks, and she and Gil started to handing them out. She was somewhat surprised to see that Hank Adamson had joined the swim again—she'd gotten the impression that he was doing each of the resort's activities just once so he could give an assessment of it.

He shrugged sheepishly when she smiled at him. "I actually like this a lot," he told her.

"I'm glad."

"Getting close to the dolphins…well, it's a whole new experience for me. Their eyes are fascinating. It's almost as if they're amused by us. They're kind of like…wet puppy dogs, I guess."

"Much bigger and more powerful when they choose to be," she said.

"Your dolphin swim is the best program here," he told her.

"Thanks."

That day, she let Gil give the introductory speech. In the middle of it, she saw Laurie Smith at last, hurrying to the platform.

A sense of relief swept over her. She realized that, deep in her heart, she had been secretly fearing, that Laurie had disappeared—that she, too, would float up somewhere in the water as a corpse.

She frowned at Laurie, but Laurie looked chagrined enough already. And Alex wasn't about to question her here.

"You're all right?" she asked Laurie briefly as her friend came up next to her.

Laurie nodded, but the look she gave Alex was strange.

"What's wrong?" Alex demanded.

"Nothing. Well, everything. Not with me, though.

And we've got to be quiet. People are looking at us. And what I have to tell you… We need to talk alone."

Alex couldn't help but whisper, "I was worried about you. Where have you been?"

Laurie gave her a look again, indicating that it wasn't the time or the place. "You have to swear to keep what I say quiet."

"You know I will, if I can."

"Not if you can. You have to listen to me. And you can't say a word," Laurie whispered. "I mean it. Not a word."

"As long as you're all right. And you're not about to tell me something that will endanger the dolphins or anyone else. Where have you been?"

"Hiding out," Laurie said.

"Why?"

"There was a corpse on the beach that day. Definitely."

"How do you know?"

"Because there's an undercover Federal agent on the island."

"What are you talking about?"

Laurie didn't get a chance to answer.

"All right," Gil announced loudly. "Time to split into groups. Those of you who received green tags with your flippers, head off with Alex and Mandy. Mandy give a wave, so your people see you. Those of you with red tags, you're with Laurie and me."

"Later," Laurie whispered. "We've got to talk. People are being murdered here." She hesitated, seeing that the groups were forming and she needed to hurry. "You've got to watch out for David, Alex."

"Watch out for David? I thought that you liked him."

"Yes, I do, but…he has a lot at stake. He…he might be the murderer."

"What?" Alex said.

"Shh! We'll talk," Laurie said. "Alone, Alex. We have to be alone."

Before Alex could stop her, she was up and heading off with Gil. Without creating a scene, there was nothing Alex could do.

Stunned, she watched Laurie walk away and pondered what she'd said. David? A murderer? It couldn't be.

Could it?

Chapter 9

"This was really kind of you," Ally Conroy told David. "I hadn't realized what a big deal you are until I started talking with Seth the other night. That you would take time for us...well, it's very kind of you." She was sitting at the helm by David. Zach, filled with excitement, was standing by the mainsail, looking out at the water as they skimmed over it.

"Not a problem. Zach is good kid."

She sighed. "Yeah, at heart. I've had some trouble with him at school. I'm a nurse, and gone too often. But...we've got to live. Anyway, thank you. I was horrible last night, and you were great. It's just, Seth might have been a blowhard to others—I've heard that term a dozen times from people talking about him—but he was very sweet to me. I was just stunned and upset. He really had a high regard for you, by the way. He was going to speak to you about something important. He said that he was waiting for the arrival of one more professional friend, then you'd all be getting down to business."

"And he talked about the Anne Marie?" David pressed gently.

She sighed. "He asked me not to say a word to anyone, but I guess it doesn't matter now. He told me that all his life, he had been interested in treasure hunting. People always wanted his money for their expeditions, but they didn't want him to be a part of them. The woman he was expecting was going to let him go along, not just foot the bills."

"Ally, did he know anything more about where this friend he was waiting for obtained her information?"

"An old man who died. He told her he'd hidden a copy of an old pirate map on this island."

David arched an eyebrow. "You're certain? There's an actual map, and it's hidden here?"

Ally sighed. "I'm not certain of anything, but that's what he said. That the ship went down off Florida, and that the map, the proof, was hidden here."

"Thank you, Ally, for telling me," David said gravely.

"Seth didn't know where the map was," she said. "That's part of why he was so concerned that his friend hadn't arrived yet. He didn't want to talk about it with you until she did arrive." She hesitated. "Do you think maybe…someone thought he knew more about the map than he did, so they killed him? Wouldn't that put you in danger, as well?"

"Ally, we don't know how Seth died yet. And I'm a pretty big boy, but I'll watch out, okay? Thanks to you."

She smiled, turning to watch her son. "Maybe you're right."

"Ally, if you think of anything else that Seth said before he died, will you please let me know?"

"Of course."

"And watch out for yourself, too. You haven't mentioned this to anyone else, have you?"

She shook her head.

"Don't—unless you're speaking with Sheriff Thompson. He'll be over here sometime today."

"I won't say a word," she promised.

He nodded and slowed the *Icarus*, shouting to Zach that he was going to lower the anchor, because they were out of protected waters and could do a little spearfishing.

Moments later, he stood aft with Zach, assuring himself that the boy could handle the speargun without skewering either himself or David. "We come back on board after every fish," he told Zach.

"Right. Because of the blood and sharks. And there are a lot of sharks out here, right?"

"Yup. They usually mind their own business, but..." He shrugged. "I had a friend once who liked to stay down and try to get a lot of fish at once. He used his swim trunks for a storage area. If a shark did smell the blood, the first place it would attack would be..."

"Ouch!" Zach said, laughing.

He tousled the kid's hair, pressed his own mask to his face and made a backward dive into the water.

He meant to give Zach his day out on the boat. He was anxious, however, to return to the dock at Moon Bay before noon. Before Alex would be out of the public eye.

Before she could be alone anywhere…

With anyone.

When the swim was over, Alex rewarded her dolphins with some pats, praise and fish, then stood, anxious to hurry over to the next platform and accost Laurie.

She didn't get a chance to. Jay, in another one of his handsome suits, came hurrying along the dock.

"We're starting evacuation proceedings now," he told her.

"Now?"

She looked at the sky. It was an unbelievably beautiful day, the sky an almost pure blue.

"Don't even bother looking up. You know how fast things can change."

"The storm turned toward us?"

"The Middle Keys may get a direct hit as early as late tonight or tomorrow morning. She's not a big one, but…well, you know. A storm is a storm. The ferry is here, and the guests are packing up. I'd like you and Gil to take a walk down to the beach and make sure we haven't missed anyone."

"Sure."

"The others can rinse down the equipment and get this part of the operation closed down. Later, if the storm keeps on coming, you can go down and open the lagoon gates so the dolphins can escape to the open sea if necessary."

She nodded. The lagoons were fairly deep; her charges could ride out a storm much better than people could. Still, the facility had been planned with escape routes for the animals, should they be needed.

"Did they act strangely today?" Jay asked.

"No."

"Then I'd say we've still got plenty of time."

Jay didn't have a particular affinity for the animals, but he knew enough about them to know that the dolphins would know when the storm was getting close.

"I see that Laurie arrived fine," Jay said.

"Yes."

"She told Len she forgot to charge her cell phone."

"Well, yesterday was her day off, and she wasn't that late this morning," Alex reminded him. Until she had a chance to listen to Laurie, she certainly didn't intend to tell Jay that anything was wrong in any way. She turned around, looking toward the next lagoon. Irritated, she realized that both trainers were already off the platform.

"Where's Gil? Does he know we're going on a beach hunt?"

"I just passed him. He's at the Tiki Hut, grabbing a sandwich."

"Is Laurie with him?"

"I don't know," Jay said. "Don't worry, you'll have a chance to talk to her when you get back. You know the island better than anyone else, so I appreciate you doing this yourself with Gil."

"Sure, I'll go find him."

Alex looked around for Laurie as she walked the path to the Tiki Hut, which was almost dead quiet, despite the time of day.

"Grilled chicken," Gil announced to her, lifting a wrapped sandwich. "I got you one, too, and a couple of bottles of water."

She arched an eyebrow, amused. "The beach isn't that far."

"Yeah, but we've got a lot of trails to check, just to make sure. The ferry's already picked up anyone who planned to check out today. It will be returning soon."

"Where did Laurie go so quickly?" Alex demanded. "She should be cleaning the equipment and battening down with Manny and Jeb."

"I don't know. She was with me right after the swim. She was pretty upset, though. She couldn't believe Jay had us finish the swim when there had been an evacuation notice. But she knows her responsibilities, and we've still got hours to get out, though I'm sure the roads will be a mess. We'll find her when we get back. Jay said you're staying, but that the rest of the dolphin team has to be on the next ferry."

"Amazing, isn't it?" she said, looking at the sky, despite the fact she knew it didn't really mean anything.

"Always a calm before a storm. Didn't your folks teach you that?" Gil teased.

"I suppose."

They reached the beach. As far as the eye could see, it appeared to be empty.

"Well, I'm sure Jay will make sure all the guests and employees are accounted for," Gil said. "But I guess we have to comb the trails anyway, huh?"

She smiled. "You go to the left, I'll go to the right, and we'll circle around and meet in the middle. How's that?"

Even as she spoke, she felt a lift in the breeze. It was subtle, but there. "I guess the storm really is coming in," she said.

"You never know. They can predict them all they

want, but that doesn't mean they're going to do what they're supposed to. Had it reached hurricane status yet?"

"I don't know," she said ruefully. "I wasn't really paying attention. Yesterday was quite a day, if you'll remember."

They'd reached the fork in the trail. "You go your way, I'll go mine," he told her.

She nodded and started off.

The trails were actually really pretty. She didn't know how many of the trees were natural and how many had been planted to give the feel of a lush rain forest. Great palm fronds waved over her head, allowing for a gentle coolness along the walk and, she noted, a lot of darkness and shadow.

The fronds whispered and rustled, and she felt as if the darkness was almost eerie, all of a sudden. There was a noise behind her, and she spun around, then felt like a fool. The noise was nothing more than a squirrel darting across a path.

Still, she felt as if she had come down with a sudden case of goose pimples, and then she knew why. David had told her not be alone.

And certainly not alone walking down an isolated trail.

She was suddenly angry. She'd never been afraid here before. She had enjoyed the solitude that could be found on the island.

But that had been before people started dying.

She quickened her steps, anxious to get back to Gil. "Hello? Anyone out here?" she called. There was no reply.

Birds chattered above her head.

She looked all around herself. Not much farther and she would meet back up with Gil.

She reached the farthest point, seeing the sand on the southern tip of the isle, and stepped off the trail to look around and call out. Nothing.

She turned back, noting that the breeze was growing stronger. In the shelter of the trees, though, she could barely feel it. The dive boat hadn't gone out that morning, she thought, but pleasure craft had probably been rented out. She hoped all the guests were back in.

"Hello?" she called out again, and once more paused to look around. She quickened her pace, then stopped suddenly.

And it wasn't a sound that had caused her to stop. It was a stench. A horrible stench.

And she knew what it was. The rotting, decaying, stench of death.

She started walking forward again, shouting now. "Gil! Gil!"

She started to run, and the smell grew stronger.

There was no denying it. Very near them, hidden in the foliage, something—or someone—lay dead.

"Gil!"

She nearly collided with him.

"What the hell is it?" he asked.

"Something dead," she told him.

"Yeah…that's what I thought. But where is it coming from?" Gil asked.

"It's gotten stronger as I've come toward you," Alex told him.

"Then it's here somewhere."

She stood still, surveying their immediate surroundings.

"Alex."

"What?"

"Let's get out of here," Gil said.

"Gil, we can't. We have to find out what it is."

"Or who it is," he said uneasily. "Alex, this is a matter for the sheriff."

"No! Yes, I mean, but not now. I am not letting anyone else disappear."

"What are you talking about?"

"We have to find out what it is, then call the sheriff. Gil, please?" Alex said. She took a few steps in the direction of a large clump of trees.

"Alex..." Gil said.

"It's here," she whispered. "There are a bunch of palm fronds on the ground, fallen leaves...and the smell is really strong. It's here."

He looked at her, then sighed. "All right. I'll lift the fronds."

"We'll do it together," she said.

They steeled themselves against the smell of death and set to work.

And after a moment, it was Gil who let out a sick croak of sound.

David had listened to the radio warnings and decided it was time to head back in. The water where they were was about seventy feet deep, and he'd snagged a few snapper. Zach, proudly, had speared his first fish ever, and it had been a beauty. Someone would be enjoying his catch tonight, one big beaut of a dolphin—or Mahi Mahi, as the restaurants called it, afraid that otherwise diners would think they were serving big cuddly marine mammals.

They hadn't taken the spearguns down this time; they'd just gone for a last look around. Far below them, a few outcrops of coral welcomed all manner of sea life.

David was just about to motion Zach back to the boat when he saw something that caused him to pause. Anemones could create the appearance of heads with waving hair, and that was what he was certain he was seeing at first. But then…

David thought there was something beneath the skeletal arms of the coral.

He surfaced, and Zach did the same, lifting his mask and snorkel. "We have to go back, huh?"

"Yes. Head on to the *Icarus*. I'll be right with you."

He watched Zach swim back to the *Icarus* was not more than twenty feet away. Then, taking a deep breath, he jackknifed in a hard, clean dive toward the depths.

He reached the coral, saw the outstretched arm, and…

Horror filled him so completely that he almost inhaled a deadly breath.

There she was.

Alicia. Or what remained of her.

Hair billowing in the water…

Features partially consumed.

Feet encased in concrete.

"That has to be the biggest, fattest, deadest possum I've seen in my entire life," Gil said, turning aside. "Phew."

"Thank God it's just a possum," Alex said fervently.

Gil looked at her, puzzled. "Okay, I know I was acting a little weird, but you seemed convinced we were going to find a person."

She shrugged, remembering that Gil had no idea she'd already found one body on the beach. "I guess I'm just spooked because of yesterday. Let's head back."

David docked the *Icarus* just long enough to drop off Ally and Zach, then headed for dry dock on the Gulf side of Plantation Key.

There he waited for Nigel Thompson to pick him up in his patrol car.

David slid into the passenger seat, meeting Nigel's gaze.

"You're a fool, you know, going back when everyone else is evacuating. Actually, I think it's about to become mandatory. You could have taken that yacht of yours and sailed her straight north," Nigel said.

"And wound up chased by the storm anyway," David said. "And you know damn well I would never leave Alex—or Moon Bay, for that matter—until this thing is solved. I hope this storm comes in and out fast."

"I'd have divers out there now, if I could," Nigel said. "But I've got every man on the evacuation route, and since we're talking about a corpse, I can't risk living men on a recovery mission. The water is getting rougher by the minute."

"I'm afraid that by the time the storm has passed through, the body might have…hell, it might have been ripped apart," David said.

"You know there's nothing I can do right now," Nigel said firmly.

David was silent, then said, "I know. But damn the timing. There was no way to get her to the surface, and then, hell, I had a kid on the boat."

"You know the location. You won't forget?" Nigel said.

"Oh, you bet I know it. And I gave you the coordinates."

Nigel glanced at him. They were on the main road at last, just miles from the ferry platform that serviced Moon Bay, but they were creeping along. There was one road down to the Keys, and one road back, so with the exodus going on, traffic was at a crawl.

"You know, Jay Galway can refuse to let you stay," Nigel warned him.

"He won't," David said with assurance.

"And you're certain you want to stay?"

"More so than ever," David said firmly.

Nigel was quiet again, then said, "Just because you found Alicia Farr today, that doesn't mean that her remains were ever at Moon Bay. I questioned everyone about the woman yesterday, when I was asking who might have seen Seth Granger leave the bar. And not a one of them saw her, any more than they did Seth."

"Which just goes to show you that no one in the place is observant. And that someone is lying," David told him. "Did you get the M.E.'s report back on Seth, yet?"

Nigel nodded.

"And?"

"The man drowned."

"I still think someone helped him do it."

Nigel twisted his head slightly. "Maybe."

"You know more than what you've said," David accused him.

"There are some bruises on the back of his skull," Nigel said. "The M.E. hasn't determined the source of them. He might have hit his head or something. Look, they took him up to Miami-Dade. One of the best guys they've got there is working on him, all right? They deal in fact, not supposition."

"Yeah. Well, there's one dead man for certain, and I know for a fact that Alicia is dead and rotting. And fact. She didn't just drown or have a boating accident. Not unless she lived long enough to cast her feet in cement and throw herself in the water."

"All right, David, I swear, the minute I've got an all clear on the weather, I'll be out there myself with the boys from the Coast Guard, hauling her up. All right?"

"I don't know if that will be soon enough," David muttered.

"For what?"

"She was murdered—there's a murderer loose. On Moon Bay. Can't you do something? I need to get back there fast."

"What do you want me to do, plow down the cars?"

"Put your siren on."

"This isn't an emergency."

"Maybe it is."

Nigel sighed, turned on his siren and steered his patrol car onto the shoulder of the road. "If I get a flat, you're fixing it."

David shook his head, offering him a half smile. "If you get a flat, I'm going to hitch a ride in the first Jeep I see."

Still on edge, Alex and Gil returned to the resort area just as the ferry was about to leave with the last of the guests and personnel. Dismayed, Alex ran to the dock, looking for Laurie.

"Alex, you're coming?" Jeb called to her from the crowded deck.

"No, but I need to see Laurie," she called from the dock.

"She's inside somewhere," he said. "I'll find her."

Gil had run up behind her. "Damn, I hope someone got my stuff." He turned to her. "You sure you want to stay? The dolphins will be just fine. Think about it, alone in that little place with Jay, Len and a handful of others? C'mon! Just hop on board the ferry. We'll have fun in Miami."

"No, no, I can't leave," she told him.

"It's going to be like a paid vacation."

Jeb came back to the rail. "Hey, Gil, I got your wallet and an overnight bag for you."

"Great."

"Where's Laurie?" Alex asked.

"She said she was coming," Jeb said.

Alex watched nervously as the ferry's ties were loosed and she prepared to depart. She scanned the vessel for Laurie. Gil barely made it to the gangplank. An impatient seaman yelled at him, "I called an aboard five minutes ago!"

"Sorry," Gil said.

The plank was up. Alex stared at the ferry in disbelief, ready to throttle Laurie herself. How could she say what she had—then disappear without a word?

Then, just as the ferry moved away from dock, Laurie appeared at last. She looked distressed. "Alex, stick with Jay, all right? Stick with Jay and Len and…whoever else."

Alex stared back at Laurie, then whipped out her cell phone, holding it up so that Laurie would see her intention.

Laurie gave her a smile, digging in her bag for her own phone.

Then she frowned and put her thumb down. "No battery!" she shouted.

"Jeb, give her a phone!" Alex shouted.

Jeb did, and a minute later Alex's phone rang. She answered it. "Laurie, what the hell's going on?"

"Alex, don't hang around David, okay?"

"Why?"

"Because something is going on. Something that has to do with salvage. Listen, you should be all right. Hank Adamson is staying on—he wants to write a story about battening down for a storm, and John will be there, too."

"John Seymore? Why?"

"I told you about him."

"No, you didn't."

"He's the agent I told you about. He's FBI. Well, I assume he's FBI. Or working with them or something."

"Laurie, how do you know this? Please, explain before the weather comes in and the phones go completely."

"All right, I'm trying. I ran into him, so we went to his cottage and talked. Just talked. That was it. I swear."

"I believe you," Alex said. "Please, get to the point."

"John said he liked you a lot, but he wasn't stepping in when there was obviously something still going on between you and David. He was concerned, though, and wished you weren't still emotionally involved with David. John's afraid that Alicia Farr has disappeared. And that she's met with foul play. He was worried about me, and he's very worried about you, because apparently there's a nurse in Miami who heard Daniel Fuller talking about you, a treasure and the dolphins. Honestly, Alex, I can see why you had such a crush on John—before David showed up again. John is wonderful. I stayed at his place—just in case anyone knew I'd seen the body you discovered and thought that I might know who it was or talk. That's why you couldn't get hold of me. I stayed there even when he was out on David's boat. And last night…he told me about Seth Granger, and that he didn't think Granger died by accident. So…he knows I was going to talk to you. Alex…Alex…are you there?"

"Yes, I'm here. Why does he suspect David?"

"Who else was close to Alicia Farr? Who else is famous for his treasure hunting expeditions? Really, you should have gotten off the island. Maybe you still can. Oh, and, Alex…"

Her voice faded, and there was a great deal of static on the line.

"Alex, did you hear me? Watch…" Static. "I know because…" Static.

Then the line went dead completely.

An arm slipped around her shoulders, and she nearly jumped a mile.

"Hey!" It was Jay. He'd actually doffed his suit and was in simple jeans and a red polo shirt so he could help batten things down. "You all right?"

"Yes, of course." She wasn't all right at all, but she sure intended to fake it. "Jay, who is still on Moon Bay?"

"There's Len and me, you, the reporter—Hank Adamson. He's been incredibly helpful, and he wants to write about the storm. It's not going to be that big a hurricane, at least."

"Right. Hopefully, she'll stay small. But who else is here, Jay? Anyone?"

"John Seymore—and your ex–old man."

"You let those two stay—and made your staff evacuate?"

"David has hit storms like this at sea, he can surely weather it. And John Seymore was a SEAL. They both wanted to stay. I had the power, and I said yes. Do you have a problem with this?"

Yes.

But she couldn't explain that she doubted both men—or why. She couldn't forget her conversation with Laurie. John Seymore claimed to be some sort of agent, but was he really? Had Laurie seen any credentials?

And what about David? David, who kept warning her that she was in danger.

Had he known she had found a body on the beach because he had been the one to murder the woman?

No, surely not. She winced, realizing that she was refusing to believe it because she was in love with him. She had been since she had met him. The divorce hadn't really meant anything, and she would probably be in love with him the rest of her life.

However long, or short, a time that might be.

Where the hell was Alex? John Seymore wondered. Jay Galway had said that he'd sent her and Gil out to check the trails, but they should have been back long ago.

He went out in search of them himself.

For a small island, there were an awful lot of trails. He began to understand what had taken them so long.

As he walked, he was easily able to assure himself that everyone else had gotten off the island. He called out now and then, looked everywhere and didn't find a soul.

But, returning, he smelled a foul odor on the air and instantly recognized it. The smell of death.

As he hurried forward, his heart shuddered hard against his chest. He stood still, looking around for any sign of company.

After a moment, convinced he was alone, he stepped forward to examine the source of the odor.

A moment later, he stepped back, relieved to have discovered only a dead possum, then hurried along the rest of the trails. When he reached the Tiki Hut, it was empty. Walking around to the docks, he saw no one, and far out to sea, the last ferry was just visible.

He turned, hesitating for a moment. Alex might have gone to the lodge. But though the winds had picked up a great deal, growing stronger by the minute now, so it seemed, they were still hardly in serious weather.

He heard a distant splash.

The dolphin lagoons.

With quick steps, he hurried toward them. He arrived in time to see Alex on the second platform, talking to her charges and handing out fish. He started along the path to the platforms. Halfway there, she met him, empty fish bucket in her hand. She stopped short, staring at him.

"Alex." He said her name with relief.

She still looked at him suspiciously.

"Alex, you…you have to be careful."

"Yes, I know," she said, sounding wary. Then she stiffened. "I hear you're an agent."

"You hear I'm what?"

"An agent. A government agent. An FBI man—or so Laurie assumes."

“I’m not on the payroll, but yes, I work with the FBI.”

“If you’re working for the government, then why not just announce it?”

“Because there are those who shouldn’t know—just yet. Because I don’t know what has really happened—or might happen.”

“So you’re accusing David of being willing to kill to get what he wants?”

John Seymore sized her up quickly and shook his head. “I’m not accusing anyone of anything. Not yet. But Alicia Farr has disappeared. And a man died under mysterious circumstances yesterday. Your name was mentioned by a dying man who supposedly held a secret worth millions.”

“I see…. So I shouldn’t trust David, and your only interest in me was because a dying man kept saying my name?” she asked skeptically.

He sighed, feeling his shoulders slump. “I want to protect you.”

“Gee, everybody wants to protect me.”

“Alex, you know that my interest in you was real.”

“What I know is that there are six of us together here for a storm. Together. I won’t be alone. And by the way, I don’t know a damn thing about the treasure, where it is, or what it has to do with dolphins, so you don’t need to draw me into casual conversation about it.”

“Alex, I really am with the authorities.”

“Want to show me some credentials?”

He pulled out his wallet, keeping his distance, showing her his identification.

“Consultant, right,” she said with polite skepticism.

“I’m a civilian employee, working special cases.”

"This is a special case?"

"I was a navy SEAL. This is a sea-related investigation."

"Well, as we both know, IDs can be easily faked."

"I'm telling the truth," he said.

"So you went after Laurie?" she said, still polite, but her tone conveying that she didn't believe a word.

"I didn't go after Laurie. There was nothing personal between us. Besides, you were back with your ex-husband," he said flatly, then added a careful, "And far too trusting of him, far too quickly."

"Well, rest assured, I'm not sure if I trust anyone anymore. And now I see Jay. I have to lock up a few things and get up to the lodge. Excuse me, please."

She walked by him as if she had all the confidence in the world. His eyes followed her, and he could see that she hadn't been lying. Jay Galway was there.

Was he to be trusted?

There was little else he could do but hurry back for his own things and get to the storm room to join the others.

He looked at the sky just as the rain began.

Chapter 10

As soon as David got back to Moon Bay, he raced to look for Alex at the dolphin lagoons. The dolphins were swimming around in an erratic manner, but there was no sign of Alex.

He decided that she might have gone to her cottage. Jay had ordered that the six of them remaining on the island had to gather in the storm room by ten that night, when the worst was due to hit, but it was nowhere near that late, and she might well have gone to her cottage for a bath, clothing and necessities.

But she wasn't at the cottage when he arrived. Running his fingers through his hair and taking long, jerky strides, he went through the little place, room by room.

Then he heard the door open and close. He hurried from her bedroom, relief filling him.

“Alex!”

“Hey,” she murmured. She didn’t sound hostile, just tense—and wary.

“Are you all right?” he demanded.

She frowned. “Of course.” She eyed him up and down. “You don’t look too good.”

“Yeah, well, I’ve been worried about you. I told you to stay in a crowd.”

“I was with someone all day,” she said, still watching him carefully. “I’ve been busy…just opened the lagoon gates. Uh, I think I need a shower. So if you’ll excuse me…”

Was she suggesting that he leave her? Not on her life. Maybe literally.

“I’ll be right here. Hey, want coffee? Tea? The electricity will probably go out soon. Of course, there’s a generator in the storm room. I guess it’s not like you can’t have tea later, if you want. But I think I’ll make some coffee, anyway.” He turned his back on her, walking to the kitchen area, reaching into the cupboard. He could feel her watching him. It wasn’t a comfortable feeling.

After a minute, he heard her walk to the bedroom. Her behavior was disturbing. She wasn’t fighting him or arguing with him—it was almost as if she were afraid to.

She reappeared just a minute later, obviously perplexed.

“When did you get here?” she asked him.

“About two minutes before you walked in. Why?”

“Did you…move things around in here today?”

“No, why?”

“Oh, nothing. The maids seem to be getting a little strange, that’s all. The maid’s been in, right? Bed is made, towels are all fresh,” she said.

"Then the maid must have been in. I didn't clean up," he said without apology.

She shrugged and stared at him. Studied him. As if she could find what she was looking for if she just kept at it long enough.

"All you really all right?" he asked her.

"I'm fine. But you really look like hell."

"I need a shower, too. I took Zach and Ally out on the *Icarus*. Then I took her around to the dry dock on the Gulf side and had to get back here."

"You didn't have to get back here," she corrected him. "You don't work here."

"I knew you'd be staying with your dolphins, and I wasn't about to leave you here alone with… Alone."

She nodded. Suddenly, to his surprise, she walked up to him, put her arms around him and pressed against him. Instinctively, he embraced her, smoothing back her wet hair. "What is it?" he asked, at a loss.

"I do know you, don't I?" she whispered.

"Better than anyone else," he said. "Alex, what is this?"

She pulled away slightly, a strange smile on her lips. "You're not good husband material, you know."

That hurt. "You were the best wife any man could have," he told her.

"You do love me, in your way, don't you?"

"In my way?" he said, finding it his turn to seek an explanation in her eyes. "In every way," he said, passion reverberating in his tone, his words vehement. "I swear, I never stopped loving you, Alex. Never. I would die for you in a heartbeat."

She slipped from his arms. "I have to shower," she murmured. "Get a few things together."

She walked into the bedroom. Five minutes later, he couldn't stand it anymore and followed.

The water was streaming down on her. Here, as in the other bath, the glass doors were clear. He should give her space, so that she wouldn't decide to send him away. Now, when he needed so desperately to be with her.

You look like hell, she had told him.

Hell yes. Because I found your disappearing body, and it is Alicia Farr, and, oh God, what the sea can do to human flesh…

There was no way he would tell her about his discovery now. Not until the storm had abated and the sheriff had come. They were all alone here now, at the mercy of the storm. And maybe of a murderer.

Her head was cast back as she rinsed shampoo from her hair. Back arched, limbs long, torso compelling in its clean-lined arc. He felt the sudden shudder of his heart and the iron tug on his muscles.

Taking a step forward, he opened the glass door. She looked at him and waited.

"I told you, I need to shower, too."

"There is another shower."

"But you're not in it."

He was startled to see her smile. Then her smile faded and a little shudder rippled through her. She backed up, inviting him in. He stripped in seconds and followed her.

"Shampoo?" she offered.

"That would be good."

"On your head?" she asked.

"Where else?"

"Should I show you?"

Her tone was absolutely innocent, and still strange.

And then he realized that she wanted him—and was afraid of him.

He set the shampoo down on a tile shelf and took her into his arms, ignoring the blast of the hot water on his shoulders. “Alex, what’s wrong?”

“I’m in danger. You told me so yourself,” she assured him, eyes amazingly green in the steamy closeness of the shower.

“But not from me,” he whispered.

She stared back at him. Then, suddenly, she shuddered once again, moving into his arms. He held her there while the water poured over them. He felt the delicious surge of heat sluicing over his body, felt himself becoming molten steel, abs bunching, sex rising, limbs feeling like iron, but vital, movable….

She knew his arousal. Knew it, sensed it, touched it. Her fingers slid erotically down the wet length of his chest and curled around his sex. She ran her fingers up and down the length of him, creating an abundance of slick, sensual suds. Spasms of arousal shuddered through him, and he lowered his lips to her shoulder, her throat, then caught her mouth with his own, tongue delving with sheer erotic intent. He ran his hands down her back, massaged his fingers over the base of her spine, cupped them around her buttocks and drew her hard against him. He was only vaguely aware of the pounding of the water. He was keenly cognizant of the feel of her flesh against his, and the heat rising between them. Catching her around the midriff, he lifted her, met her eyes and slowly brought her down, sheathing himself inside her, and finally, when her limbs were wrapped around him and they were completely locked together, he pressed her back against the tile and began to move. She buried her head against his neck, rocking, riding, moving with his every thrust, her teeth grazing his shoulders, the water careening over them both. It wasn't enough.

Without letting her go, he used one hand to reach for the door. Opening it, he exited the slick shower with her still enfolding him and staggered to the bedroom, then fell down on the bed with her, drenching the neat spread and not caring in the least. They rocked together in a desperate rhythm that seemed to be echoed by the rise of the wind and spatter of the rain beyond the confines of the cottage. He moved, and his lips found her throat, her breasts, her mouth, once again. He brought them both to a near frenzy, withdrew, and then, despite her fingers in his hair and her urgency to bring him back, he kissed the length of her soap-slicked body, burying himself between her thighs, relishing her words of both ecstasy and urgency, at last rejoining her once again, his force rising with his shuddering thrust, until they climaxed in a sweet and shattering explosion.

They lay together afterward, damp and panting. His arm remained around her, but strangely, she suddenly seemed detached. So passionate, so incredible…

And then…

"It's getting late. I've got to get dressed. Grab a few things…did you want to go to your cottage? You could do that while I pack a few things."

He stared down at her, definitely taken aback. "Wham, bang, thank you, sir?" he inquired politely.

She flushed. "There's a storm on the way."

"Of course, excuse me, let me just get out of the way."

He rose, baffled, heading for his clothes. Then he stopped, turning back to her. "Alex, there's always a storm on the way."

"What are you talking about?"

"You—there's always something. You won't talk."

"There is a storm out there!" she exclaimed.

"If you'd ever called me, ever talked about the thoughts going through your mind—"

"I called you a number of times, David. There was always someone there to say that you'd get back to me, you were in the water, you were working with a submersible...you were...well, God knows what you were doing," she told him.

He started to walk back toward her. Strangely, she backed away from him.

"David, there is a storm out there. And worse," she added softly.

"We both should have gotten off the island," he said angrily, and started to leave again. Then he spun back on her, letting her edge away from him until she came flat against the bedroom wall. Then he pinned her there.

"Get this straight. Whatever you're feeling, whatever I did, whatever you think I did, I would defend you with my last breath, I would die to keep you safe, and I will love you the rest of my life. Turn your back on me and never see me again when this is over, hell, don't even send a Christmas card, but for the love of God, trust me now!"

He didn't wait for a reply. She had been too passionate, then too stubborn and distant, for him to expect a response that made sense. It was as if she had suddenly decided that she didn't trust him.

He was dressed before she was, wearing the swim trunks and T-shirt he'd had on all day. In a few minutes she was dressed as well, a small duffel bag thrown over her shoulder. "I thought you were getting your things?" she said.

"I'm not leaving you," he told her. "Come on; we've got to stop by my place."

The wind had really picked up, and rain was pelting down. Alex started out, then stepped back, telling him she had macs in the cabinet. They were bright yellow. They certainly wouldn't be hiding in those, David thought grimly.

When he opened the door again, the wind nearly ripped it from its hinges. "Let's go!" he shouted. "This thing is coming in really fast."

They ran along the path. Thankfully, David's cottage was close. Inside, he didn't bother dressing, just grabbed fresh clothing and toiletries, then joined Alex again in minutes. They started along the trail toward the lodge. Just as they neared the Tiki Hut and the lagoons, a flash of lightning tore across the sky, almost directly in front of them.

They heard a thunderous boom. Sparks seemed to explode in the sky.

The island went dark, except for the generator-run lights from the lodge.

In the dark, David took her arm. Together, they began to hurry carefully across the lawn to the main lobby, where Jay was waiting for them impatiently.

He led the way through the reception area, the back

office and through a door that led down several steps. It wasn't a storm cellar, since it would be impossible to dig on an island that had been enhanced by man to begin with. Rather, the ground had been built up, so they were actually on a man-made hill.

The storm room was just that—one big room. There were ten cots set up in it, others folded and lined up against a wall, and doors that were labeled "Men" and "Women." There was a large dining table, surrounded by a number of upholstered chairs, and a counter that separated a kitchen area from the rest of the room. A battery-operated radio sat on the counter.

"Nice," David commented.

"Very nice," Hank Adamson said, rising from where he'd been sitting at the foot of one of the cots. "It's great, actually."

"If you like being closed in," Len said, shrugging. It was clear that he had remained only out of deference to Jay. But he offered a weak grin.

"The kitchen is stocked, we've got plenty of water, and as you can see, the generator has already kicked in," Jay said. "The brunt of the storm is due at about 4 or 5 a.m. She's still moving quickly, which is good. And her winds are at a shade less than a hundred miles an hour, so she's not a category four or five."

"With any luck, it will be all over by late tomorrow morning," Len said.

"And the damage, hopefully, will be minimal," Jay said. "The trees, though…and the foliage. They always go. No way out of it, we'll have one hell of a mess."

"But here we all are," Hank said cheerfully. "So…what do we do?"

John Seymore had been in one of the plush chairs, reading a book. His back had been to them. He rose. "We can play poker," he suggested. "Someone saw to it that there are cards, chips, all the makings of a good game. There's even beer in the refrigerator." He was speaking to everyone in the room, but he was staring at David.

David assessed him in return. "Poker sounds good to me," he said.

"Right," John said. "We can see just who is bluffing whom."

"Sounds like fun," Hank Adamson said. "Deal me in."

Outside, the wind howled. The sound of the rain thundering against the roof was loud, and Jay had turned the volume high on the radio to hear the weather report.

The poker game continued.

It might have been any Friday night men's crowd—except Alex was playing, too. She liked poker and played fairly well. But in this group...?

They'd set a limit, quarter raises, no more. And yet it seemed that every round the pot got higher and higher.

Neither John nor David ever seemed to fold, or even to check. Between them, they were winning eighty percent of the time. When one of them dealt, there were no wild cards, and it was always five-card stud. Their faces were grim.

Thank God for Len and Jay. As the deal came around to Jay for a second time, he shuffled, calling his game. "Seven cards. One-eyed Jacks and bearded kings wild."

"One-eyed Jacks and bearded kings?" John Seymore said, shaking his head.

"What's wrong with that?" Len asked defensively. "Adds some spark to the game."

"I think our friends are used to hard-core, macho poker," Hank Adamson said, grinning at Alex across the table.

"Sounds like a fine game, right, John?" David asked.

"You bet," John said.

There was a slight discrepancy over one of the kings—whether he actually had a beard or if it was only five o'clock shadow. It was Alex's card, and she said she didn't need for it to be wild. For once, she had a hand. A royal flush, with the king being just what he was.

It seemed to be the only hand she was going to take. Watching David and John, she had a feeling they would both do well in Vegas.

It was difficult to sit there. She wondered how she could have spent the time she had with David, how she could have gone to her cottage, felt the overwhelming urge to make love, while still feeling that little tingle of doubt. But watching John Seymore and the subtle—and not so subtle—ways he challenged David, she had a difficult time believing that he could be an out-and-out liar or a murderer, either.

Jay's third turn to deal, and he called for Indian poker.

"What?" David asked.

"You must have played as a kid. We all get one card and slap it on our foreheads. We bet on what we think we have," Jay explained. "You can try to make faces, bluff each other out."

"It's fun, do it," Alex advised.

The cards went around, and they all pressed them to their foreheads, then stared at one another.

"Hey, there aren't any mirrors in here, are there?" Hank Adamson asked.

"Don't think so. And no one is wearing glasses, so we should be all right."

"What do we do now?" John asked.

"You're next to me. You make the first bet," Alex said.

John shrugged and threw in a quarter chip.

He had a three on his forehead. Jay had a seven; Len had the queen of diamonds, Hank a ten, and David the queen of hearts. "Big bet, buddy, for a guy with your card," Len warned him.

"Oh, yeah?" John said. "You should fold right now."

"You don't say? My quarter is in."

"You really should fold," David told John.

"You think? I'm pretty sure you shouldn't even have bothered to ante," John told him.

Betting went around twice, with each of them saying some things that were true and others that weren't.

In the end, Len folded, followed by Hank, and then Jay. The pot rose, and Alex was amazed in the end to find out that she'd been sitting with the Queen of Spades on her head, enough to beat David's queen of hearts.

"I don't think I should play against you guys. You're going to lie about every hand, and I'm going to fall for it," Len said.

"Len, at most, you're going to lose about twenty-five dollars tonight," Alex told him. "Start bluffing yourself."

"I never could lie," he murmured, shaking his head.

"Ah, an insinuation that the rest of us can lie with real talent?" Hank asked him.

"Careful—anything you say can and probably will be used in a column," Alex warned Len.

"Hey, I'm wounded," Hank protested. "Seriously, I'm having a blast, and I'm going to write this place up as the next paradise."

"Let the man win a few, will you, guys?" Jay said, pleased.

"Yeah, Alex, quit winning," Len said.

"Me? Look at those two," she said, indicating the piles of chips in front of David and John.

"Right. Quit winning, you two," Jay said.

"Hey! I can bluff with the best of them. Don't anyone dare let me win," Hank protested.

"Storms are funny, huh?" Len said a few minutes later, passing the cards to John. "My sister's in-laws all have boats and live right on the water. Years ago, Andrew was supposed to hit the coast. They all asked to come in and stay with my sister inland. Well, that's where the storm came in, and they all got mad at her when their cars were flattened and they had to spent the night praying in a bathtub! This is better, huh?" he said to no one in particular.

"Who would have figured we'd be here tonight?" Jay said, shrugging.

"Who'd have figured?" David echoed. He was staring at John.

"Yeah, odd isn't it, how the best-laid plans can be interrupted by nature?" John Seymore responded.

It was enough for Alex. She had to get away from the table and all the dueling testosterone or she was going to scream.

She yawned. "I'm going to beg out of this. I'm going to make a cup of tea, and then I'm going to sleep."

"But you just won a huge pot. That's not legal," Len said.

"You can split my pot among you. I think I can spring for the ten bucks," she told him, pushing her pile of chips toward the center.

"I can cash you out," Jay said. "That's not a problem."

"And not necessary. Quit worrying and take the chips." Grinning, Alex left them. She walked to the kitchen area, amazed that the storm could be raging all around them, the electricity was out—probably all through the Middle Keys, at the least—but thanks to the generator, she still had the ability to see and make tea. She turned up the radio and heard the newscaster. They were taking a pounding. It could have been much worse, if the storm had been able to pick up more speed.

"Anyone else want anything?" she called, expecting them to ask for a round of beers.

"Naw, thanks," Jay said.

His polite refusal went all around. Alex found it very strange. Poker and beer always seemed to go together, along with an assortment of snacks. None of these guys wanted anything.

It was as if they were all determined to keep a totally clear head.

The game continued as she made her tea. Though on the surface it appeared as if they were just playing cards, she had a feeling that for John and David, it was much more. They challenged one another at every turn.

She sipped her tea, half listening to the game, half to the radio. In a minute, she was going to try to sleep. When she woke up, the storm would be over. The islands would be in a state of wreckage, but hopefully, it would be more trees and foliage than homes and buildings.

But what then? Would she finally get a chance to talk

to Nigel? Would they find the truth behind Seth Granger's death?

And what about Alicia, the treasure and the dolphins?

She finished the tea and stretched out on one of the cots. Her eyes closed, then opened suddenly.

Because someone in the room was doing a great deal more than bluffing at poker. Alicia Farr was dead. And Seth was dead, and…

Very likely, someone in the room had committed murder.

David.

No.

Why would he kill Alicia? He had plenty of money from his own enterprises. Of course, he spent it, too. His excursions were costly, and not everything he did was financed by a major corporation. But why kill Alicia? He couldn't go after treasure alone.

And she herself was still in love with him. No matter what had happened, she'd been eager to sleep with him again. Even now, she was sure he was using her. She was apparently the key to something, somehow. Damn Daniel Fuller, even if he had passed on! Why had he dragged her into this?

Then there was John Seymore. Claiming that he, too, had come to protect her. Said he was working with the FBI, even had a great-looking ID. And hey, why not try to seduce the woman he was there to protect? He'd used her, too. But until she'd talked to Laurie tonight, she had liked him, really liked him. And she'd believed he was genuinely interested in her, too, because her instincts had said so.

So much for instincts.

And now…

How could she trust either of them?

She was never going to get to sleep.

"Hey!"

She jumped at the sound of Jay's voice. She rolled over to look at him. He was listening intently to the radio.

"We'll be in the eye of the storm in about half an hour."

He was right. Listening, Alex realized that the brutal pounding of wind and rain was easing somewhat.

"When it comes, I wonder if I should take a peek at the damage," Jay said.

"It's going to be the same damage in the morning," David advised him.

"Yeah, but we'll have at least twenty minutes before it starts up hard again," Jay said.

"This storm is a fast mover," David reminded him.

"He's losing. He just wants to opt out of the game himself for a few minutes," Len said.

"I think we'll all be opting out in a few minutes," Hank said. "Looking at our sleeping beauty over there, I'm feeling the yawns coming on myself."

"We should all get some rest," David said. "I have a feeling it's going to be a real bitch around here after it lets up."

"It will take a few days to get our little piece of the world up and going again, sure," Jay said. "Depending on the damage the main islands face. They'll have electric crews out first, then road crews…we'll have people out next. It's just a matter of repair and cleanup. We've done it before, we'll do it again."

"Actually, I wasn't referring to the storm damage," David said.

"Oh?" Jay said. "Then what?"

"Nigel was supposed to be coming out today to talk to people about Seth Granger," David said.

Len exhaled a snort of impatience. The others must have stared at him, Alex thought, because he quickly said, "Look, I'm sorry. I don't know if it's the right term for a man or not but he was one hell of a prima donna. He thought money could buy him anything, and he was rude to anyone he thought was beneath him. He drank like a fish. If he hadn't drowned, he would have died soon of a shot liver anyway. I'm sorry a man is dead. But I can't cry over the fact that he got drunk and fell in the water."

"But what if he didn't just fall in the water?" David said.

"You were all there with him. What the hell could have happened? He stepped out for air, lost his balance and fell into the drink. Case closed."

"I'm not sure Nigel sees it that way," David said. "Besides, there's more."

"And what would that be?" Jay asked, groaning.

"Oh, come on, Jay. We all know Alicia Farr was supposed to be here. I have the feeling Hank never really came here to do a story on the island. He was hoping to find Alicia and get the lead on whatever she knew," David said.

"You certainly came here to find Alicia," John told him politely.

"Yeah?" David said. "You supposedly didn't even know her—but I'm willing to bet you came here because of her, too. And maybe you actually found her."

"What the hell does that mean?" Len asked.

No one answered him.

"You know, David, you've sure as hell been acting strange today. Starting out your day with the mom and the kid, then dropping them off and moving your yacht."

"He dry-docked his yacht," Jay put in. "If I had a vessel like the *Icarus*, I'd damn sure do the same thing."

"But he came back," Len noted, his tone curious, as he studied David.

"Did you find something out in the water today?" Jay asked. "Is that why you're acting so strange?"

Hank's voice was eager. "Oh my God! You did. You found…oh my God!" he repeated. "You found the body! The body that disappeared from the beach."

"No!" Len exploded. "You couldn't have! This is getting scary. Bodies everywhere."

"Where did you find the body?" John Seymore asked sharply.

"Another drowning victim?" Jay asked, sounding confused.

"I don't think so," David said. "I sure as hell didn't mean to bring this up during the storm, but since it seems you're all going to jump to conclusions, anyway, I might as well tell you the simple truth. No, not a drowning victim. Drowning victims aren't usually found with their feet encased in cement."

Where she lay, Alex froze.

"This is quite a story," Hank said.

Jay groaned. "You just had to bring this up in front of Hank, right, David?"

"I didn't bring it up!" David said sharply. "But maybe it doesn't matter. When the storm is over, the news will break anyway. As soon as he can, Nigel is sending someone out to bring her up."

"Where did you find the body?" Hank asked.

"Out beyond the reefs. I was spearfishing with Zach. Couldn't bring it up myself, because I didn't have the equipment to bring up any weight. Plus I'd already pushed the envelope on getting the kid and his mom back in, and the *Icarus* out of the storm. Nigel couldn't send anyone right away, because his people were all involved in the evacuation, and the water was growing too dangerous, too fast. But once the storm has passed, he'll get the Coast Guard in and bring her out."

"Jeez," Hank breathed.

"Did you know her?" Jay asked.

"Yes, I did. It was Alicia Farr," David said.

The moan of the wind outside was the only sound then as every man at the table went dead silent.

"Alicia Farr—dead," Hank Adamson said at last.

The others turned to stare at him, and he continued, "All right! I did come out here to get a story on her. I'd heard she was on to some incredible find."

Alex heard something make a clunking sound. She turned to look, but quietly, not wanting them to know she was awake, not when she was chilled to the bone just listening.

The clunking sound had been made by Jay as he allowed his head to fall on the table. She was sure it wasn't an emotional response to a woman being dead, though, and maybe she couldn't blame him. He hadn't really known Alicia Farr.

He was worried about Moon Bay.

David had known Alicia, and now Alex understood why he had been so tense.

He'd found Alicia's body.

Someone hadn't wanted the body to be found, so that someone had gone back for her, hidden her, then packed her in cement and thrown her back in the water, sure that this time she wouldn't wash back up.

Had that someone been David, and was he saying this now just to cover his own actions? Of course, he could find the location of the body, because he had put it there himself. The timing was certainly in his favor if he had. The storm could move the body, hide it, even destroy it. The cause of death might become almost impossible to discern. Any physical evidence could be completely compromised.

No, David couldn't be a killer. She wouldn't believe it. He had his talents, but he had never claimed acting to be among them.

And yet, at that table, they had all been bluffing.

Anger against herself welled in her heart. No, how could she believe in her soul that she loved someone so much that she had been so afraid of losing him that she had pushed him away, and then believe him capable of deception and murder?

"On that note, I think the game is over," John murmured. "Hell, I can't believe you kept quiet until now."

"I meant to keep quiet all night," David said irritably. "There's nothing anyone can do until the storm passes. Then the body will be brought up, and Nigel will get to the bottom of what's going on."

"Maybe," Jay said dully. "And maybe he won't find out a damn thing and we'll all be walking around afraid forever."

"I don't think so," David said. "I'm pretty sure that whoever killed Alicia might have helped Seth Granger into the water. And that person will, eventually, give himself away. Until then, just be careful."

"Great, David, thanks a lot," Len said. "Now none of us is going to be able to get any sleep."

"Why?" David said. "Hey, it's just the six of us on the island. We stick together, nothing goes wrong," he said flatly.

A strained silence followed his words.

"No one sleeps, that much is evident," Len said at last.

The sound of the wind suddenly seemed to die out completely.

The eye of the storm was just about on them.

"Hell," Hank Adamson swore. "This is ridiculous. I'm going to sleep. Alicia Farr is dead, and you found her," he told David. "That doesn't make any of us guilty of anything. You're right. Tomorrow, or as soon as he can, Nigel will come out and take care of things."

He pushed his chair away from the table. Alex kept her eyes tightly closed, not wanting any of them to know she had heard their conversation.

"We're in the eye," Jay said suddenly. "Len, come with me. I'm going out. Just for a minute. Just to take a quick look around." He sounded strained.

"You shouldn't go out, Jay," David said.

"I have responsibilities here. I have to go out," Jay said. "The rest of you stay here. Len will be with me. Everyone will have someone keeping an eye on them."

"Just you and Len together?" John said.

"All right, then. Three and three. Hank, you come with us for a minute," Jay said.

Hank groaned.

"Please. Three and three," Jay repeated.

With a sigh, Hank rose and joined them. Jay unbolted the door, stepping out into the dim light of the world beyond the shelter. "We'll just be a minute."

Alex didn't believe for a minute that he was going out to check on the damage. They kept a gun in a lockbox behind the check-in counter. He was undoubtedly going for it.

"What the hell are you doing on this island?" David asked John.

"The same back to you," John said.

Then, out of the blue, the radio went silent as the room was pitched into total blackness.

Chapter 11

The hum of the generator was gone.

Something had gone terribly wrong.

For a moment David sat in stunned silence, listening to the absolute nothing that surrounded him in the pitch darkness. Then he heard a chair scraping against the floor.

John Seymore. The man was up, and Alex was sleeping on a cot just feet away. Seymore could be going after her. Fear—maybe irrational, maybe not—seized him. He couldn't seem to control his urge to protect Alex, no matter what.

He sprang up, hearing the scrape of his own chair against the floor. He heard movement, tried to judge the sound, then made a wild tackle, going after the man.

He connected with his target right by the row of cots. His arms around his opponent's midsection, together they crashed downward, onto the cot where Alex had been sleeping.

Dimly, as Seymore twisted, sending a fist flying, David became aware that the cot was empty. Alex had fled. She might still be in the storm-shelter room somewhere, or she could have found the door and escaped.

Seymore's fist connected with his right shoulder. A powerful punch. Blindly, David returned the blow. He thought he caught Seymore's chin. The man let out a grunt of pain, then twisted to find David with another blow.

They continued fighting for several minutes with desperate urgency, until suddenly an earsplitting gunshot rocked the pitch-dark room.

Both of them went still. The shot had come from the doorway.

Instinctively, they rolled away from one another.

"Alex!" David shouted.

There was no answer.

After the explosion of sound, silence descended again. He wasn't sure where Seymore had gone.

With a sudden burst of speed, he picked himself up and raced toward the open door. Insane or not, instinct compelled him to do so.

Alex was certain that John and David were going to tear each other apart. Damn Jay! They were supposed to stay together, watching one another, and instead he'd gone for a weapon. What the hell did he intend to do? Hold everyone at gunpoint until the authorities came? Shoot them all?

Could Jay be the killer? No! She refused to believe it. And yet… As soon as he'd left, the generator had gone off.

What the hell had happened?

She had no idea. All she knew for certain was that David and John had suddenly become mortal combatants. Did they know something she didn't? Was one of them telling the truth—and the other not?

She had to get away, in case the wrong man triumphed. Not that she had any idea which one was the wrong one.

She'd already deserted her cot before they toppled over on it. She immediately made a dash for the door, nearly killing herself in the process, the darkness was so complete. She burst into the office and stood dead still, listening. Once she was certain the office was empty, she made her way to the reception area, inch by inch, using the furniture as a guide.

She meant to head for the lockbox herself, just in case she'd been wrong and Jay hadn't gone for the gun after all. Then became aware of breathing near her. She held dead still, holding her own breath.

Waiting, listening.

Aeons seemed to pass in which she didn't move. She nearly shrieked when she realized someone was moving past her, heading for the storm room. Once he had gone and her heartbeat had returned to normal, she tried to move around the reception counter.

Her footsteps were blocked. She kicked against something warm. Kneeling, feeling around, she realized that she hadn't stumbled against a thing but a person.

She recoiled instantly, fought for a sense of sanity, and tried to ascertain what had happened—and who it was. The form was still warm. She moved her hand over the throat, finding a pulse. Feeling the face and clothing, she decided she had stumbled upon Jay Galway, and he was hurt!

Either that, or…

Or he was lying in wait. Ready to ambush the unwary person who knelt down next to him to ascertain what had happened.

Fingers reached out for her, vising around her wrist. She screamed, but the crack of a gunshot drowned out the sound. She wrenched her wrist free and rose, determined to get the hell out of the lodge. The storm might be ready to come pounding down on them again, but she didn't care. There had to be a different place to find sanctuary.

As she groped her way out of the lodge, tamping down thoughts of Jay and whether or not he was hurt or dangerous, she was certain that her survival depended on escape. She lost several seconds battling with the bolts on the main door, then got them open and flew out.

Everything in her fought against believing Jay was the killer. He definitely hadn't been the one shooting the gun.

If Jay was on the floor, where were Len and Hank?

This was all insane!

The night was dark. Thick clouds covered the sky, even in the eye of the storm. Still, once outside, she could see more than she had before.

She hurried along the once manicured walkway, heading not toward the dock but around to the Tiki Hut, on the lodge side of the dolphin lagoons.

As she rushed forward, she was aware of a few dark dolphin heads bobbing up.

She never passed without a giving an encouraging word to her charges. Despite the darkness, she was certain the dolphins could see her, and they would instinctively know something was wrong when she didn't acknowledge them.

She should say something to them.

She didn't dare.

She was determined to make her way to the cottages. Not her own—that would be the first place anyone would look for her—but she was sure she would find a door that hadn't been locked. The cottages were nowhere near as secure as the storm room, but at least they'd been built after Hurricane Andrew and were up to code.

But as she veered toward the trail that led toward the cottages, she saw another form moving in the night ahead of her.

Panic seized her. There was no choice. She had to head for the beach.

She turned, then heard footsteps in her wake.

She was being pursued.

David was desperate to get to Alex. He damned himself a hundred times over for the announcement he had been forced to make. For not beating the crap out of Jay, rather than letting him leave the room.

But had Jay—or anyone—destroyed the generator? Or had technology simply failed them when it was most desperately needed?

Didn't matter, none of it mattered.

Out of the room, he stumbled, swearing, as he made his way through the inner office and out to reception.

He hesitated. Somewhere on the wall was a glass case that held a speargun. It was a real speargun, one that had been used in a movie filmed on the island a few years earlier. He'd passed it dozens of times, giving it no notice.

Now he wanted it.

Groping along the wall, he found the case. He smashed the glass with his elbow, grabbed the weapon, then heard movement behind him.

David streaked for the front doors, praying that nothing would bar his way.

He found the door, which was slightly ajar.

Yes, Alex had definitely gone outside.

He swung the door open, leaving the lodge behind.

It occurred to him to wonder just how much time had passed since the eye had first come over them.

And just how much time they had left.

There had to be a way to double back and find a place to hide and weather the storm.

Alex ran along the path toward the beach, then swore. There was no branch in the trail here, but if she crawled through the foliage, she could reach one of the other paths. All too aware that someone was following and not far behind, she caught hold of an old pine tree and used it for balance as she entered into the overgrowth.

Already, much of it was flattened. Even if she had found a path, it wouldn't have been worth much. The storm had brought down hundreds of palm fronds already. Coconuts, mangoes, and other fruits littered the ground. She tried to move carefully, then paused, wondering if she had lost her pursuer.

She stood very still, listening.

She could hear the sea. The storm might not be on

them again yet, but the water was far from smooth. She could hear the waves crashing, could imagine them, white capped and dangerous. And beneath the water's surface, the sand and currents would be churning with a staggering strength.

Had the wind begun to pick up again yet?

Footsteps.

Whoever had been behind her was pursuing her now with slow deliberation, as if he was able to read the signs of her trail in the dark. Maybe he could.

Who was he? Had Jay been an enemy, just waiting in the darkness, or a victim? If not Jay, who could it be?

She froze in place, stock-still with indecision. Which way to go?

There was a rushing in her ears. Her own pulse. She ignored it. She had to listen above it.

Yes, there was another sound in the night. Footsteps, not the beat of her own heart.

Her pursuer. Close. Too close.

As silently as possible, she edged forward, then came to a dead stop once again. There was a new noise, coming from in front of her.

Where to go?

Only one choice.

She headed toward the beach.

She was ahead of him, so close it was as if he could still smell her perfume, on the air. And still she was eluding him.

She knew the island, and he didn't.

David didn't dare call out her name. Someone else might hear him. Once again, he damned himself for the bombshell he had dropped that night. Now the killer knew. He had hidden Alicia's body and now he knew he'd failed a second time. For a moment his mind wandered to the spot where he'd found the body. It wasn't an area where he had believed it would be found, where dive boats brought scores of people daily, but it wasn't impossibly far from the beaten path, either.

So what did that mean? What did the placement of the body mean?

He couldn't worry about it now. He had to use every one of his senses to find Alex.

Before it was too late.

He paused and listened. The rustle of the trees was eerie in the strange breeze that gripped the island. It was as if the storm was gone…and yet still there.

She was moving again. The sound was so slight, he nearly missed it. He started tearing through the bushes again, following.

She was heading for the beach.

He saw her as she raced forward, then stumbled and fell. Seconds later, he burst out of the bushes behind her.

"Alex!"

He saw then what she was seeing. Just feet from her, Len Creighton was facedown in the sand. In the night, David couldn't make out anything else, whether the man was injured, unconscious…dead.

He couldn't see Alex's reaction to her discovery, but he could tell she'd heard him. She was on her feet again, and she was staring at him, and even in the dark, he could see the fear in her eyes.

"Alex!" he cried. "Alex, come here."

She kept staring at him. As he waited, afraid to move

closer, lest she run again, he surveyed the area as best he could in the dark.

Where had Len come from? How had he gotten here?

Where was the danger?

He stared at Alex again. "Alex, you've got to trust me. Come with me—now. Quickly!"

He was dimly aware of leaves rustling nearby; he knew someone else had reached them even before he heard a deep voice protest, "No!"

John Seymore. Damn. He'd been on his trail the whole time. Now, David realized, he'd led the bastard right to Alex.

John Seymore stared at David with lethal promise. He had a gun. Apparently he'd been armed all along and never let on. He could kill the other man, and he knew it. But whether or not he could kill him before David sent a spear into his heart was another matter.

"Alex!" Seymore shouted, keeping a wary eye on David. "Come to me. Get away from him."

"Alex!" David warned sharply.

It seemed as if they stood locked in the eye of time, just as they were locked in the eye of the storm, forever.

Alex stared from one man to the other, and back again. Her gaze slipped down to Len Creighton, who was still lying on the beach, then focussed on the two men once again.

Then she turned and dived straight into the water.

"Alex, no!" David shouted.

He couldn't begin to imagine the undercurrents, the power of the water, in the wake of the storm. And he didn't give a damn about anything other than getting her back. He even forgot that a bullet could stop him in his tracks in two seconds. He dropped the speargun and went tearing toward the water.

A dim line barely showed where water and sky met. As he plowed into the waves, he saw something shoot through the water. For a moment he thought Seymore had somehow managed to move quicker than he had and had gotten ahead of him in the violent surf.

Then he realized that whoever was ahead of him was huge, bigger than a man. David plowed on, fighting the waves to reach Alex, heedless of who else might be out there. He broke the surface.

Then he saw.

Alex was being rescued. And not by a man, not by a human being at all. One of her dolphins had come for her. Where the animal would go with her, he didn't know.

"Alex!" he screamed again.

But she had grabbed hold of the dolphin's dorsal fin, and the mammal could manage the wild surf as no man possibly could.

She was gone.

He treaded the water, watching as the dolphin and the woman disappeared in the night. The danger hadn't abated in the least; it was increasing with every minute that went by. He was losing to the power of the water himself. Fighting hard despite his strength and ability, he made it back toward the beach. When he reached the shore, he collapsed, still half in the water.

A second later, someone dropped by his side.

Seymore. Apparently he had ditched his weapon, as well, equally determined to rescue Alex from the surf.

Both men realized where they were and jerked away from one another. Then both looked toward the weapons they had dropped. David could see Seymour's muscles bunching, and he knew his were doing the same.

But Seymore cried out to him instead of moving. "Wait!"

David, wary, still hesitated.

"You had plenty of time to kill her," Seymore said.

"You could have shot me," David noted warily.

"You'd have shot back. But the point is...you dropped the speargun and went after Alex."

"Of course I went after her! I love her."

Seymore inhaled. "Listen to me, I didn't kill anyone. I know you think it's me, but I'm working with the FBI—"

"Yeah, yeah, sure. Now you're a G-man."

"No, I'm a special consultant. I thought *you* were killing people—until two minutes ago."

David found himself staring at the man. His basic reaction was to distrust him, but there was something about the man he believed. Maybe the fact that the Glock had been a guarantee, the speargun a maybe.

Seconds ticked by. Alex was in the care of a creature that could survive the darkness and the elements better than any man. But she was still out there somewhere. And the greatest likelihood was that the dolphin would bring her back to the lagoon. It wouldn't take the animal long.

There was also the matter of the man lying on the beach just feet away from them, possibly dying.

"I'm not the killer," Seymore said.

"And neither am I," David said harshly. More seconds ticked by.

Gut reaction. Dane had told him to go by his gut reaction.

He let another fraction of time go by. Then he moved.

Ignoring Seymore, he got to his feet quickly and walked over to the prone body of Len Creighton. There was blood on the man's temple, but he still had a pulse.

"He's alive," David said. Hunkered down, he tried to assess the man's condition quickly. Concussion, almost certainly. Shock, probably.

If they left him there, he would certainly die in the next onslaught of the storm. But if he was burdened with the man, Alex could die before he got back to her.

David's back was to Seymore. The man could have picked up the gun and shot him, but he hadn't.

David turned back to him. "He's got to be taken to shelter."

Seymore picked up the gun, shoving it into his belt. He stared at David, but, like him, he knew that time was of the essence.

"Alex is out there," John said.

"Yes."

"She'll trust you before she trusts me, though she doesn't seem to have much faith in either of us at the moment," he said at last. "Go after Alex. I'll take Len." Then, true to his word, he bent down, lifting the prone man as if he were no more than a baby.

David hoped to hell the guy was really on his side. As an enemy, he would be formidable.

Was he wrong? Was this all part of an act. Were they all supposed to die tonight, but on Seymore's own terms? He might be leaving Len to face instant death.

There wasn't time to weigh the veracity of John Seymore's words.

"Cottage eight was Ally and Zach's. It's probably open," David said.

"Meet me there," John Seymore said briefly.

There was nothing left to do. David turned, scooped up the speargun, and started running back toward the Tiki Hut and the dolphin lagoons.

At first Alex had thought she had signed her own death warrant. It wasn't that she didn't know the power of the waves. She'd been out in bad weather before. She'd seen people flounder when the waves were only four feet. She couldn't begin to imagine how high they were now, but desperation had driven her into the water.

Even with everything she knew, she still hadn't imagined the battering she was going to take, the impossibility of actually swimming against the force of the sea.

She had thought she was going to die.

Then she had felt the smooth, slick, velvet sliding by her. Her mind had been too numbed at first to comprehend. The animal had made a second glide-by, and then she had known.

When Shania returned for her that time, she was ready, catching hold of the dorsal fin, just as she taught tourists to do on a daily basis.

She caught hold, though, and knew that she was doing it for her life. Still, despite her fear and panic and the waves and the desperation of the situation, she was awed. She had heard stories about dolphins performing amazing rescues. She worked with them on a daily basis, knew their intelligence and their affection.

And still...she was in awe. For a moment she wondered where the dolphin would go, and then she knew.

Safe haven.

The dolphin lagoon. Shania's home, the place where she found shelter. Where she had gone when she had been sick and injured. Where she had been nursed back to health.

The dolphin moved with astounding speed. As they neared the submerged gates to the first lagoon, Alex was afraid that she would be crushed against the steel. Shania had more faith in her own abilities. She dove low with her human passenger and raced through the opening, and they emerged in the sheltered lagoon.

"Sweet girl, sweet girl, thank you!" Alex whispered fervently to the dolphin, easing her hold and stroking the creature. "I owe you so many fish. I won't even slip vitamins into any of them," she promised.

Soundlessly, Shania moved off. Alex swam hard to the platform, crawling out of the water, shaking.

She was cold, soaking wet, barefoot, and no better off than when she had begun.

The winds would whip up again, and she had not found shelter.

Out there, somewhere, were two armed men. David and John.

And then there was Jay.... Would he have left Len to die on the sand? Oh God, she'd forgotten in her panic. And Hank? Where had he gone?

Her heart felt as numb as her fingers. There was nowhere to go, and no one to trust.

What the hell to do now? She started to rise, but a sudden wind gust nearly knocked her over. The storm was on its way back.

She headed back around the lagoon, creeping low,

her goal now the Tiki Hut. The bar was solid oak. If she wedged herself beneath it, with any luck she would survive the winds and get only a minimal lashing from the rain.

Another gust of wind came along, pushing her forward. She was going to have to wedge herself tightly in. She could and would survive the night, she promised herself.

But when morning came…what then?

David raced along the path, pausing only when he neared the lagoons, trying desperately to see in the darkness. The rain was becoming heavier; the wind had shifted fully and was now beginning to pick up speed.

Trying to utilize the remaining foliage for cover, he searched the area surrounding the lagoons, then the water. The darkness was deceptive, but he thought he saw dark heads bobbing now and then.

He had no idea which animal had come for Alex, how it had known she was in trouble, or where to find her. Dolphins had excellent vision; he knew they sometimes watched people from deep in the water. But how a dolphin had known where to look for Alex, he would never know.

Even though he couldn't see Alex, he was certain the dolphin had brought her back to the lagoon. Unless something had happened along the way

He wouldn't accept such a possibility.

David sprinted around the lagoons to the platforms. He felt he was being watched. He searched the closest pool, then the farther one. At the second lagoon, one of the dolphins let out a noise. He brought a finger to his lips. "Shh. Please."

Assuming that John Seymore had told him the truth, and taking into consideration the fact that Len Creighton was definitely out, there were still two more men on the island, one of whom obviously posed a deadly threat.

"Where did you bring Alex, girl?" he asked the dolphin.

Intelligent eyes stared back at him, but the animal gave no indication of Alex's direction in any way.

As he retraced the path back toward the resort, David thought he saw a movement in the Tiki Hut.

Alex?

He set the speargun down against the base of a palm, knowing that for the moment, he needed his hands free.

What if the person seeking shelter in the hut wasn't Alex?

It had to be.

And if not…he had to take the chance anyway.

Slowly, crouching low, he started to move in that direction. He crept with all the silence he could manage and with the cover of a growing wind.

There she was, seeking shelter under the bar of the Tiki Hut. A good choice.

Still, he didn't show himself. She would scream, run, perhaps make it to the lagoons, and with her animals certain she was in danger, they would protect her once again. They were powerful animals, and knew their power. They could be lethal, taking a man to the bottom of a pool, keeping him there.

He moved very, very slowly. Then froze.

There was a sound from the brush nearby.

A bullet exploded, the sound loud even against the howl of nature.

David made a dive, crashing down against Alex and

clasping a hand over her mouth before she could scream.

She panicked, tried to fight him. "Shh, Alex, it's me. You have to trust me," he mouthed as her eyes, luminous and huge, met his. She remained as tense as a stretched rubber band, staring at him.

Then another shot sounded in the night. He felt her flinch, but he couldn't release her mouth nor so much as shift his weight. If she drew attention to them now…

Forcing his weight hard against her, his hand still pressed against her mouth, David remained dead still. Listening. Waiting. It was so difficult to hear over the storm, to separate the natural moan, bend and rustle of the foliage from the sounds that were man-made.

He waited.

Then…yes. Someone was going off down one of the paths. He could hear the barely perceptible sound of receding footsteps.

He eased his hand off Alex's mouth. She inhaled fiercely, staring at him with doubt and fury and fear.

"Please, Alex," he begged. "Trust me."

Her lashes fell. "Trust you?" she whispered. "What about John Seymore? Did you kill him?"

She sounded cold, almost as if she were asking a question that didn't concern her.

"No."

"So you're not the killer? He's not the killer?"

"I don't think so."

"You don't *think* so?" she said, her voice rising.

He clamped a hand over her mouth again. "Shh."

She stared up at him with eyes of pure fire. He eased his hand away again. "Damn you, Alex, I love you. I'd die before I'd cause you any harm. Don't you know that about me?"

Her lashes fell again. "Actually, it's hard to know anything about you," she said.

That was when the lightning flashed. Struck. The boom of thunder was instantaneous, as the top of the Tiki Hut burst into flames.

For split seconds, they were both stunned.

Then David made it to his feet, seizing her hand, dragging her up. "We've got to move!" he urged. Without waiting for her assent, he dragged her quickly through the debris of branches and foliage that now littered the floor.

They headed down the trail toward the cottages as the rain began to pelt them.

"Where are we going?" Alex gasped, pulling back. "Our cottages are the first place anyone would look."

He didn't answer; the night had grown so dark again that he was barely able to make his way through the trails. All his concentration was on finding their way.

"David?"

"Shh."

He longed to pause, to listen.

He dared not.

Moments later, they reached the cottage where he had delivered Ally Conroy the night before. The door was closed, but when he set his hand on the knob and turned, David found it unlocked.

Then he paused at last.

Seymore could have been lying. The guy was military, experienced. He could kill them all off, one by one. He would never be found. Before relief crews could make it to the island, he could head out, move Alicia Farr's body once again, then disappear. He would know how to do that.

Gut instinct.

And no choice.

David opened the door.

Chapter 12

Alex blinked, colliding with David's back as he entered the cottage, then stopped dead.

She peered past him.

The darkness was broken by the thin beam of a flashlight in the kitchen area of the cottage.

They heard the click of a trigger, and a face appeared in the pale light.

John Seymore.

For a moment his features were as macabre as the eeriest Halloween mask. And for a moment she and David were as frozen as ice.

John Seymore took his finger off the trigger, shoving the gun back into his belt. "Alex. You're all right," he breathed.

"Yes," she said stiffly.

"Where's Len?" David asked.

"I've got him on the floor in the kitchen. I cleaned the wound. He's got a concussion, I'm sure. There's nothing else I can do for him now," John said.

"He's alive?" Alex breathed.

"Barely. His only chance is for us to get him across to medical care the minute we can," John said.

Alex moved around from behind David, still wary as she passed John Seymore, heading for the kitchen.

Len was stretched out there. John had covered him with blankets from the beds and set his head on a pillow. She touched Len's cheek and felt warmth. His pulse was weak but steady, his breathing faint, but even.

She sat back, leaning against the refrigerator, allowing herself the luxury of just sitting for a minute, appreciating the fact that she was alive.

Then her mind began to race. The wind was howling again. She could hear it rattling against the doors in the back. She winced, afraid they would give way, then reminded herself that they were guaranteed to withstand winds up to a hundred miles an hour.

She began to shiver, then started as a blanket fell around her. She looked up. David was standing there; then he hunkered down by her side. A minute later John Seymore sat down across from them, on Len's other side.

"Who did this to him?" Alex demanded, looking from one man to the other.

David stared directly at John Seymore as he answered. "Either Jay Galway or Hank Adamson," he said.

She shook her head. "Jay cared about Len too much."

"Did he?" John asked dryly. "Jay is the manager

here. If Alicia had ever shown up, he'd be the one to know it. Especially if she wanted to arrive in secret. Jay could have met her on the beach and killed her."

"No," Alex said. "Jay's hurt—I nearly tripped over him up at the main building, and then he—never mind. It had to be Hank."

"A reporter? Without any special knowledge of boats or the sea?" David asked quietly.

She stared across Len's still form to at John Seymore. "So…you're FBI but not exactly an agent?" There was wariness in her voice, and she knew it.

John sighed. "Look, if I hadn't been so suspicious of David, I would have identified myself from the beginning. But I didn't know who could be trusted. For all I knew, you were in on it somehow, Alex."

"What I want to know," David said, "is how the FBI became interested in Alicia Farr, and why?"

"The government always wants its cut," John said simply. "Different agencies, at different times, had their eyes on Daniel Fuller. He liked to talk. According to his stories, the ship went down in American waters. No way was the government going to let a treasure hunter get to her secretly."

"So…you followed Alicia?" David said.

John shook his head. "I'd been in Miami. We knew Daniel Fuller was dying, but he refused to see anyone but Alicia. I'm sorry she lost her life over this, but she was a fool. She didn't exactly hide her visits. She was overheard calling Moon Bay. So I came to see what would happen when she arrived. My job was just to find out what she knew about the *Anne Marie*. But Alicia didn't show up. You did, David. And Seth Granger, who talked way too much. And the reporter. Then Alex found the body on the beach."

Alex felt David's fingers curl around hers. She swallowed hard. There was something so instinctively protective in that hold.

For a moment, the gravity of their situation slipped away.

If John Seymore suddenly pulled out his gun, she knew David would throw himself between them. He *did* love her.

Maybe he had always loved her.

But the sea would always come first.

"How did you know Alex found a body on the beach?" David demanded sharply.

John shrugged. "I made a point of meeting up with Laurie Smith. She's a very trusting individual. Too trusting, really. It was risky, telling Laurie the truth. But it also seemed important that she lie low, since someone might know she had been with Alex and seen the body."

"Laurie is on the mainland, or at least the main island, if she didn't head out of the Keys entirely," Alex murmured. "So she knows. She knows everything that's going on. It's insane for someone to be trying to kill us all now. The authorities will know."

David was staring at John again. "Maybe not so insane. Whoever killed Alicia also helped Seth Granger to his death. That means they didn't care about financing. We've got someone on our hands who means to get to the wreckage of the *Anne Marie*, bring up the treasure without equipment or an exploratory party, then disappear."

Alex looked from one man to another. "All right, for the sake of argument right now, David, you've decided it isn't John, and, John, you've decided it isn't David. And it's obviously not Len or Jay." She frowned. "I told you, when I ran out of the storm room, I tripped over Jay."

"He was dead?" David asked sharply.

Both men were staring at her.

She shook her head. "No," she admitted. "He...he tried to grab me."

Their silence told her that they both believed Jay was guilty.

"He was the one who insisted on going out," David said to John.

"He'd know how to kill the generator," John agreed.

"Wait!" Alex protested in defense of her boss. "He didn't attack me. I was afraid, so I ran, but...but he could have been hurt," she said guiltily, "and just trying to get me to help him."

"Alex," John said seriously, "you know that you're the one the killer really wants. It was your name Daniel Fuller mentioned over and over again. Are you sure you don't know why?"

She felt David's tension, his fingers tightening around hers. She knew what he was thinking. If you actually know something, for God's sake, keep quiet now!

He might have decided to trust John Seymore, but John's question had set off sparks of suspicion in his mind once again.

So why did she trust David so implicitly? Maybe he had been so determined to save her because he, too, believed she knew something.

"I don't have a clue. He never talked to me about the *Anne Marie*. Ever. He rambled on, told lots of stories about the sea, and he loved the dolphins. That's all I know," she said. Her words rang with sincerity, as they should have. They were true.

"Well, hard to hide anything on a dolphin," David said. He was staring at John Seymore. Sizing him up again?

"What do we do now?" she murmured.

As if in answer, the wind howled louder.

"Wait out the storm," John said.

"You have a gun," Alex said, pointing at John. "The doors lock. We can just wait until someone comes from the main island, until the sheriff gets here. Even if the killer comes after us, well...there are three of us, not counting Len, and one of him."

"Or two," David said grimly.

John cocked his head toward David. "You think Hank and Jay are in on this together?"

"I don't think anything. I'm just trying to consider all the possibilities," David said.

"Once the storm is over, we can't really sit around waiting to be attacked, anyway," John said.

"Why not?" Alex asked.

"Because," David said, not looking at her but at John Seymore, "even if Nigel was the first one to show up after the storm, he could be shot and killed before he ever got to us. If only one man is behind this, it's likely the other one is dead already. And we know the killer's armed."

"We need a plan," John murmured.

"Whatever the plan, Alex stays here," David said. "Locked in, when we go out."

"Great. I'll be a sitting duck," Alex murmured.

"Locked in," David repeated sternly.

"And what are you two going to do?" she demanded. "This isn't a big island, but there are all kinds of nooks and crannies where someone could hide. How are you going to find him—or them?"

"Well, we've got a few hours to figure it out," John said grimly. "No one will be moving anywhere in this wind."

Toward dawn, Alex actually drifted off, her head on David's shoulder. He was loathe to move her, not just for the silky feel of her head against him, but for the trust she had displayed by allowing her eyes to close while she was next to him.

Trust, or exhaustion.

"It's over," John said.

Seymore hadn't dozed off. Neither had David. They had stared at one another throughout the night. Now it was morning, and the storm was over.

They had their plan.

David roused Alex. "Hey," he said softly.

She jerked awake, eyes wide.

"We're going," he told her. "Remember, you don't open the door to anyone once we've gone. Not John, and not me."

"I don't like this," she protested. "The sheriff could be far more prepared than either of you think. He's not a bumpkin. You should both stay put, right where you are. That leaves us as three against one, remember?" She was pleading, she realized.

"You'll be all right if you just stay locked in," David said.

"I'm not worried about me, you idiot!" she lashed out. "I'm worried about the two of you. Going out as if you—"

"Alex, let us do this," John said.

"Don't forget no one—*no one*—comes in," David

warned her sternly again. This was going to be difficult for Alex, he knew. She was accustomed to being the one in charge, accustomed to action.

And they were asking her to just sit tight.

"I've got it," she said wearily. "I heard you. But I still don't understand what the two of you are going to do."

"We're going back together for the speargun," David said. "Then John is going to watch the trail, and I'm going to wait at your cottage."

"You know, whoever this is could come here and we could ambush him. Or them," she tried.

"Alex, he—or they—may never realize we came to this cottage," David said. "In fact, we're praying that he doesn't."

He got to his feet. John joined him. He reached a hand down to Alex, drawing her to her feet and against him. His voice was husky when he said, "No one." He moved his fingers against her nape, sudden paralysis gripping his stomach.

Seymore looked away.

David kissed Alex. Briefly. But tenderly.

"Follow us to the door and bolt it immediately, don't just lock it," John told Alex. "If it's Jay, he's got a master key."

"Bolts, on both doors," David said. "Front and back."

"Yes, immediately," she said.

They stepped out cautiously.

The world seemed to be a sea of ripped-up palm fronds and foliage. Small trees were down all over.

"Close the door," David told Alex.

Her beautiful, ever-changing, sea-colored blue-green eyes touched his one last time. She went back in, and he heard the bolt slide into place behind them.

"This way for the speargun," he told John Seymore. The other man nodded grimly and followed his lead.

Alex's diving watch was ticking.

Five minutes, ten minutes.

Fifteen minutes.

By then she was pacing. Every second seemed an agony. Listening to the world beyond the cottage, she could at first hear nothing.

Then, every now and then, a trill.

Already, the birds were returning.

Her stomach growled so loudly that it made her jump. She felt guilty for feeling hunger when David and John were out there, in danger, and Len Creighton still lay unconscious on the kitchen floor.

With that thought, she returned to his side. He hadn't moved; his condition hadn't changed. She secured the blankets around him more tightly.

That was when she heard the shots.

She jumped a mile as she heard the glass of the rear sliding doors shatter.

Alex didn't wait. She tore through the place, closing doors so that whoever was out there would be forced to look for her. Then she raced into the front bedroom, opened the window and forced out the screen, grateful they hadn't boarded up the place. As she crawled out the window, she wondered if the shooter was Jay Galway or Hank Adamson.

Then it occurred to her that maybe they didn't know the truth about John Seymore.

And he was the only one of them who she knew had a gun.

In the stillness of the morning, the bullets hitting the glass, one after another with determined precision, sounded like cannon shots.

David had been waiting by the door of Alex's cottage. He'd left it ajar, standing just inside with the speargun at the ready as he watched the trail. No one would be coming through the back without his knowledge—he'd dragged all the furniture against it.

But at the sound of the gunshots, he started swearing. What if John Seymore was the shooter?

No, couldn't be. Gut instinct.

Someone was shooting, though, and David felt ill as he left the cottage and raced dexterously over the ground that was deeply carpeted in debris.

What if his gut instinct had been wrong?

He'd left Alex at the mercy of a killer.

Heedless of being quiet, he raced toward Ally's cottage, heading for the back door.

Instinct forced him to halt, using a tree as cover, when he first saw the shattered glass. He scanned the area, saw no one, heard no one.

Racing across the open space, the speargun at the ready, he reached the rear of the cottage.

He listened but still didn't hear a thing.

The broken glass crunched beneath his feet, and he went still. Once again he heard nothing. Slowly, his finger itchy on the trigger, he made his way in and moved toward the kitchen.

There, lying under a pile of blankets, just as they had

left him, was Len Creighton. Then, before he could even ascertain whether Len was still alive, David heard a noise, just a rustling, from the front bedroom.

Silently, he moved in that direction.

The door to her cottage was open.

Alex had run like a Key deer from the other cottage and, without even thinking about it, had come here.

Because David would be here.

The front door was ajar.

She hesitated, found a piece of downed coconut and threw it toward the open doorway. Nothing happened.

Cautiously, she made her way to the door. She peered inside. No one. Logic told her that once he'd heard the bullets, David would have run to her assistance.

She entered her cottage, thinking desperately about what she might have that could serve as a weapon. The best she could come up with was a scuba knife.

She kept most of her equipment at the marina, but there were a few things here.

She raced into her bedroom, anxious to pull open the drawer where she kept odds and ends of extra equipment, reminding herself to keep quiet in case she had been followed. But she was in such a hurry that she jerked the entire dresser.

Perfumes and colognes jiggled, then started to topple over. She reached out to stop them from crashing to the floor and instead knocked them all to the floor with the sweep of her hand.

The sound seemed deafening.

She swore, returning attention to the drawer, but then something caught the corner of her eye.

She paused, looking at the pile of broken ceramics and glass.

The little dolphin had broken, and she could see that a piece of folded paper had been hidden inside the bottom of the ceramic creature.

Squatting down, she retrieved it.

Ordinary copy paper.

But as she opened it, she realized just what had been copied. A map. The original had been very old, and there was an X on it, and next to that, three words: *The Anne Marie.*

She stared at it numbly for a second, then remembered the day when she had found her things out of order. Someone must have hidden the map that day. Returning her mind to her predicament. Rising, she opened the drawer, heedless now of making noise. She found the knife she had been seeking and quickly belted it around her calf.

Then she heard a noise as someone came stealthily toward the front of the house.

Once again, she made a quick escape through a bedroom window.

David burst into the bedroom of Ally's cottage, speargun aimed.

But no one was there.

He immediately noticed the open window and the punched-out screen lying on the floor.

Silently, he left the bedroom, then the house, and hurried on toward Alex's place.

Now the door was wide open. Cautiously, he entered. He hurried through the cottage.

This time, it was her own bedroom window that was open. A punched-out screen lay mangled on the floor.

He heard a shot.

The sound had come from the area of the Tiki Hut.

He raced from the house and toward the lagoons.

“Stop, Alex. Stop!”

She had simply run when she left her place. Away from the front door. Her steps had brought her to the lagoons and the Tiki Hut. She made it to the lagoon on the outskirts of the Tiki Hut, which was little more than a pile of rubble now. She spared a moment’s gratitude that she hadn’t spent the night under the bar after all.

The voice calling to her gave her pause.

It was John Seymore. And she knew he had a gun.

She turned, and he was there, closing in on her.

“Wait for me,” he said. But as she stared at him, another man burst from the trees.

It was Hank Adamson. And he, too, was armed.

“Alex, it’s all right!” Adamson called out. “I’ve got him covered. Seymore, put down the gun or I’ll shoot you.”

“Alex, let him shoot me,” John said. “Get the hell away from him.”

“Alex, don’t be an idiot. Don’t run,” Hank Adamson insisted.

At that moment, David burst from the foliage, his speargun raised. “Alex, get the hell away from here!” David roared, but then he paused, seeing the situation.

“Hey, David,” Hank Adamson called. “I’ve got him!”

“Yeah, I see that,” David said. For a moment his eyes met hers. Then they turned toward the lagoon before meeting hers again. She realized that he was telling her to escape. Shania had helped her once. The dolphin would surely take her away again.

But she didn't dare move.

"Yeah, you've got him, all right," David said, walking to Seymore's side. "Hank, where's Jay?" he asked. "It's all right, Alex. It's okay…Hank has got this guy covered."

She knew from his eyes that he didn't mean it.

But how was he so sure that John Seymore wasn't the bad guy?

"Hank, where's Jay?" David repeated.

"This guy must have gotten him during the night," Hank said, indicating John.

And then Alex knew. Amazingly, David looked dead calm, and earnest, as if he were falling for every word Hank Adamson said. He was gambling again, she realized. Bluffing. In a game where the stakes were life or death.

His life.

She could see what he was doing. He was going to go for Hank Adamson and take the chance of being shot. He was risking John Seymore's life, as well, but she could see in that man's eyes that he was willing to take the risk. The guy was for real.

"Now!" David shouted.

His spear flashed in the brilliant morning sunlight that had followed the storm.

John Seymore made a dive for her, and they crashed into the lagoon together.

As they pitched below the surface of the water, Alex was aware of the bullet ripping through it next to them. She heard the repercussion as another shot was fired.

In the depths of the lagoon, the bullets harmlessly pierced the bottom. She and Seymore kicked their way back to the surface. Heads bobbed around them. Dolphin heads. Her charges were about to go after John.

"No, no…it's all right!" She quickly gave them a signal, then ignored both them and John Seymore as she kicked furiously to reach the shore.

Two men were down.

"Careful!" John was right behind her, holding her back when she would have rushed forward.

He walked ahead of her.

Hank Adamson, speared through the ribs, was on top. Blood gushed from his wound.

"David!"

She shrieked his name, falling to the ground, trying to reach him as John Seymore lifted Hank Adamson's bleeding form.

"David!"

He opened his eyes.

"David, are you hurt? Are you shot?"

"Alex," he said softly, and his voice sounded like a croak.

"Don't you die, you bastard!" she cried. "I love you, David. I was an idiot, a scared idiot. Don't you dare die on me now!"

He smiled, then pushed himself entirely free of Hank Adamson and the pile of leaves and branches that had cushioned them both when they fell. He got to his feet.

"She loves me," he told John Seymore, smiling.

Seymore laughed.

Alex couldn't help it. She threw a punch at David's shoulder. "That doesn't mean I could live with you," she told him furiously.

"Actually, we have another worry before we get to that," David said, looking at John. "We've got to find

Jay. And pray that help gets here soon, or we'll lose Len for certain."

They found Jay near where Alex had stumbled into him the night before. He was groaning, obviously alive. From the doorway, they could see him starting to rise. When he heard them, he went flat and silent once again.

"It's all right, Jay," Alex said, racing to his side. "It's over."

He sat up, holding his head, fear still in his eyes as he looked at them.

"It was Hank," he said, as if still amazed. "It was Hank…all along."

"We know," Alex told him.

"Len?"

"He's alive. We have to get him to a hospital as soon as possible," John said.

"Thank God," Jay breathed. He looked at them all. "*Hank,*" he repeated. "How did you figure it out?"

John looked at David. "How *did* you figure it out?"

Alex stared at David, as well.

David shrugged. "Two things. Seth Granger was killed. The man with the money, and Hank would fit into that category. That meant it had to be someone who didn't need money or backing. Someone who meant to get what he could, then get out."

"You said two things," John Seymore told him.

David stared at John. "Gut instinct," he said at last. He angled his head to one side for a moment, listening, and said, "There's a launch coming. Thank God. Nigel Thompson can take over from here."

Epilogue

She hurried along the trail. She knew she was being pursued, but now, the knowledge brought a smile to her face.

They would be alone. Finally, after all the trauma, all the hours.

Still, there was something she had to do first.

Hank Adamson wasn't dead; he, like Jay and Len, had been taken aboard a helicopter and airlifted to Jackson Memorial in Miami. All three men were expected to make a full recovery.

It was chillingly clear that the reporter had intended to use the storm as cover to kill them all, Alex last, so that he could find out what she knew by saving one victim for the end and pretending he would let him live if she would just talk.

He would never have believed that she didn't know

anything. Until the end, of course. Before Nigel arrived, she had given the map to David, then smiled in relief when he had turned it over to Nigel Thompson.

She didn't give a damn about the whereabouts of the *Anne Marie*. And even if David did, people were still more important to him than any treasure.

She reached the first platform, and fed Katy, Sabra and Jamie-Boy, aware she was being watched.

As she sat down at the next platform, David, who had come after her, sat down beside her. "I have to butt in here," he told her. "I owe Shania, too. I owe her everything. Do you mind?"

Alex shook her head, and watched him for a moment as he fed and touched every dolphin, talking to them all, giving Shania special care.

"You know," she said softly, "I was jealous of Alicia, but I'm truly sorry that she's dead."

"So am I." He looked at her. "You were wrong, though, to be jealous. We never had an affair."

"She was just so…perfect for you," Alex said.

"No, she wasn't. I was always in love with you. *You* were perfect for me. I was an ass. I didn't show it. You loved your training, I loved the sea. I didn't know how selfish I had gotten."

"Well, since we're still married," she mused, "I guess we'll just have to learn how to compromise."

"Alex?"

"What?"

"I lied," he admitted. "I saw you with Seymore, and I had to think of something. Because this much is true. I love you, more than anything on earth, with every bit of my heart, my soul, and my being."

"You lied to me?" she said.

He shook his head, looking at her. "Alex, I've learned to never, ever take someone you love for granted. We can compromise. I don't need to be in on the find of the century. For me," he added softly, "*you* are the find of the century. Any century. Don't throw us away again, please."

"David, that's lovely. Really lovely. But are you saying we're not still married? That's what you lied about?"

"Forgive me. I didn't know what else to do. Well?"

She smiled. "Actually, I'm thinking that we should be remarried here. Right here. By the lagoons. A small ceremony, with just our closest friends here. I mean, we did the big-wedding thing already."

He gazed at her, slowly giving her a deep, rueful grin.

Then he pulled her into his arms and kissed her.

* * * * *

"Graham has crafted a fine paranormal romance with a strong mystery plot and a vibrant setting."

—*Booklist* on *Haunted*

Sometimes closing your eyes doesn't help....

Toni MacNally and her friends think they've hit on the ultimate moneymaking plan when they buy a run-down Scottish castle and turn it into a tourist destination. But when the castle's actual owner—a tall, dark and formidable Scot—returns, the group is soon drawn into a real-life murder mystery. Young women are being killed, their bodies dumped nearby. And now Toni is having sinister lifelike dreams in which she sees through the eyes of the killer....

Please turn the page for an exciting preview of

THE PRESENCE

by

Heather Graham

Available from MIRA books
September 2004

Prologue

Nightmares

The scream rose and echoed in the night with blood-curdling resonance that only the truly young, and truly terrified, could create.

Her parents ran into the room, called by instinct to battle whatever force had brought about such absolute horror in their beloved child.

Yet there was nothing. Nothing but their nine-year-old, standing on the bed, arms locked at her sides, fingers curled into her fists with a terrible rigidity, as if she had suddenly become an old woman. She was screaming, the sound coming again and again, high, screeching, tearing, like the sound of fingernails dragged down the length of a blackboard.

Both parents looked desperately around the room, then their eyes met.

"Sweetheart, sweetheart!"

Her mother came for her, unnoticed, and tried to take the girl into her arms, but she was inflexible. The father came forward, calling her name, taking her and then shaking her. Once again, she gave no notice.

Then she went down. She simply crumpled into a heap in the center of the bed. Again the parents looked at one another, then the mother rushed forward, sweeping the girl into her arms, cradling her to her breast. "Sweetie, please, please…!"

Blue eyes the color of a soft summer sky opened to hers. They were filled with angelic innocence. The child's head was haloed by her wealth of white-blond hair, and she smiled sleepily at the sight of her mother's face, as if nothing had happened, as if the bone-jarring sounds had never come from her lips.

"Did you have a nightmare?" her mother asked anxiously.

Then a troubled frown knit her brow. "No!" she whispered, and the sky-blue eyes darkened, the fragile little body began to shake.

The mother looked at her husband, shaking her head. "We've got to call the doctor."

"It's 2:00 a.m. She's had a nightmare."

"We need to call someone."

"No," the father said firmly. "We need to tuck her back into bed and discuss it in the morning."

"But—"

"If we call the doctor, we'll be referred to the emergency room. And if we go to the emergency room, we'll sit there for hours, and they'll tell us to take her to a shrink in the morning."

"Donald!"

"It's true, Ellen, and you know it."

Ellen looked down. Her daughter was staring at her with huge eyes, shaking now.

"The police!" she whispered.

"The police?" Ellen asked.

"I saw him, Mommy. I saw what that awful man did to the lady."

"What lady, darling?"

"She was on the street, stopping cars. She had big red hair and a short silver skirt. The man stopped for her in a red car with no top, like Uncle Ted's. She got in with him and he drove and then…and then…"

Donald walked across the room and took hold of his daughter's shoulders. "Stop this! You're lying. You haven't been out of this room!"

Ellen shoved her husband away. "Stop it! She's terrified as it is."

"And you're going to call the police? Our only child will wind up on the front page of the papers, and if they don't catch this psycho murdering women, he'll come after her! No, Ellen."

"Maybe they can catch him," Ellen suggested softly.

"You have to forget it!" Donald said sternly to his daughter.

She nodded gravely, then shook her head. "I have to tell it!" she whispered.

Ellen seldom argued with Donald. But tonight she had picked her battle.

"When this happens…you have to let her talk."

"No police!" Donald insisted.

"I'll call Adam."

"That shyster!"

"He's no shyster and you know it."

Donald's eyes slid from his wife's to those of his daughter, which were awash in misery and a fear she shouldn't have to know. "Call the man," he said.

He was very old; that was Toni's first opinion of Adam Harrison. His face was long, his body was thin and his hair was snow-white. But his eyes were the kindest, most knowing, she had seen in her nine years on earth.

He came to the bedside, took her hand, clasped it firmly between his own and smiled slowly. She had been shaking, but his gentle hold eased the trembling from her, just as it warmed her. He was very special. He understood that she had seen what she had seen without ever leaving the house. And she knew, of course, that it was ridiculous. Such things didn't happen. But it had happened.

She hated it. Loathed it. And she understood her father's concern. It was a very bad thing. People would make fun of her—or they would want to use her ability for their own purpose.

"So, tell me about it," Adam said to her after he had explained that he was an old friend of her mother's family.

"I saw it," she whispered, and the shaking began again.

"Tell me what you saw."

"There was a woman on the street, trying to get cars to stop. One stopped. She leaned into it, and she started to talk to the man about money. Then she went with him. She got into the car. It was red."

"It was a convertible?"

"Like Uncle Ted's car."

"Right," he said, squeezing her hand again.

Her voice became a monotone. She repeated some of the conversation between the man and woman word for word. Perspiration broke out on her body as she felt the woman's growing sense of fear. She couldn't breathe as she described the knife. She was drenched with sweat at the end, and cold. So cold. He talked to her and assured her.

Then the police arrived, called by neighbors who had been awakened by her screams. The two officers flanked her bed and started firing questions at her, demanding to know what she had seen—or what had been done to her.

Despite the terror, she had felt all right because of Adam. But now huge tears formed in her eyes. "Nothing, nothing! I saw nothing!"

Adam rose, his voice firm and filled with such authority that even the men with their guns and badges listened to him. They left the room. Adam winked at her and went with the men, telling her that he would talk to them.

A month later, the police came back to the house. She could hear her father angrily telling them that they had to leave her alone. But despite his argument, she found herself facing a police officer who kept asking her terrible questions. He described horrific things, his voice growing rougher and rougher. Somewhere in there, she closed off. She couldn't bear to hear him anymore.

She woke up in the hospital. Her mother was by her

side, tears in her eyes. She was radiant with happiness when Toni blinked and looked at her.

Her father was there, too. He kissed Toni on the forehead, then, choking, left the room. An older man in the back stepped up to her.

"You're going to move," he told her cheerfully. "Out to the country. The police will never come again."

"The police?"

"Yes, don't you remember?"

She shook her head. "I'm sorry...I'm really sorry. I don't know who you are."

He arched a fuzzy white brow, staring at her. "I'm Adam. Adam Harrison. You really don't remember me?"

She studied him gravely and shook her head. She was lying but he just smiled and his smile was warm and comforting.

"Just remember my name. And if you ever need me, call me. If you dream again, or have a nightmare..."

"I don't have nightmares," she told him.

"If you dream..."

"Oh, I'm certain I don't have dreams. I don't let myself have dreams. Some people can do that, you know."

His smile deepened. "Yes, actually, I do know. Well, Miss Antoinette Fraser, it has been an incredible pleasure to see you, and to see you looking so well. If you ever just want to say hello, remember my name."

She gripped his hand suddenly. "I will always remember your name," she told him.

"If you ever need me, I'll be there," he promised.

He brushed a kiss on her forehead, and then he was gone. Just a whisper of his aftershave remained.

Soon her memory faded and the whole thing became vague, not real. There was just a remnant in her mind, no more than…that whisper of aftershave when someone was really, truly gone.